The Last Kings 2

The Last Kings 2

C.N. Phillips

www.urbanbooks.net

Urban Books, LLC
300 Farmingdale Road, NY-Route 109
Farmingdale, NY 11735

The Last Kings 2 Copyright © 2017 C.N. Phillips

ISBN 13: 978-1-62286-772-1
ISBN 10: 1-62286-772-6

First Trade Paperback Printing January 2017
Printed in the United States of America

10 9 8 7 6 5 4 3 2 1

This is a work of fiction. Any references or similarities to actual events, real people, living or dead, or to real locales are intended to give the novel a sense of reality. Any similarity in other names, characters, places, and incidents is entirely coincidental.

Distributed by Kensington Publishing Corp.
Submit Orders to:
Customer Service
400 Hahn Road
Westminster, MD 21157-4627
Phone: 1-800-733-3000
Fax: 1-800-659-2436

The Last Kings 2

C.N. Phillips

Acknowledgments

To Ryiann. My beautiful baby girl. I have loved you since the first time I heard your heartbeat. I knew I was bringing you into a world with nothing to offer you, so now it's my duty to give you the world. You have the purest soul and are the most beautiful person that I know. The happiness you bring to my life is all that a mother could ever ask for, and to you I give all thanks. You are and have always been my greatest motivation, and every book I write will be dedicated to you. No matter what I do, you always end my days with your beautiful smile, even when you're mad at me. That only comes from that unconditional, real love. Your loyalty is unmatched. If you learn anything from me being your mother, I want it to be to follow your dreams. Never be afraid to go after what you believe in, because your dreams are the things that nobody can take from you. I love you always and forever, Tink!

To A Marie. You have been more than just a cousin to me, you are the Marley to my Mike. The Yin to my Yang. The sugar to my iced tea—okay, okay I'll stop dragging it! Ha! But seriously, I don't know what I would do if I couldn't pick up the phone and call you. Or if you weren't in my life for that matter! You are truly my rock. Whenever I was close to hitting rock bottom you never let my feet touch the ground, and that is exactly what a Day One is supposed to do. We have always been there to support and love each other, and I know we are going far.

Acknowledgments

Everyone deserves that one person in their corner who never left, and for me it's you. That is why you are my daughter's Godmom. Thank you . . . for everything!

To Ja'Von, where do I start? Oh, yeah, best fraaannnnn! Oh my goodness, I feel like I've known you my whole life. I know we get on each other's backs like sisters, but we have each other's backs like them too. We coparent together and I love that our daughters get to grow up together like sisters too. We go through the same things, which is awesome, because that means we always will have each other to lean on. We cry together (because we're both soft thugs), but it feels good to be able to talk to you about *everything*. We talk about our kids and our futures often. You told me to put in your acknowledgment, "Make sure you tell them that I'm single, I'm a freak, and I like dark-skinned men." LOL! You are so crazy, but such a beautiful person inside and out. You have a kind heart and would never let anyone you care about go without, and for that you deserve the world. Love you best friend!

Last but most definitely not least: to you all, the readers! If it weren't for you, this dream . . . this vision of mine wouldn't be able to be made possible. Thank you all so much for supporting me and allowing me to share my thoughts and my words with you. Thank you for welcoming the crazy worlds that are inside of my head into yours. I hope that you enjoy all of my past, present, and future work whenever you pick up something I created. You are all absolutely amazing! Now, without further ado, I would like to present you the follow up to my freshman novel, *The Last Kings*. Enjoy!

Prologue

Don Rivera sat in the living room of his mansion in Azua, Dominican Republic watching the flames dance inside of his fire place. In his hand he held a glass of scotch, and his thoughts consumed him. As the leader of the Dominican Cartel, one would assume that he had everything he wanted, but he knew something was absent from his life. He yearned for the family he once had, but his selfishness led him to choose the world of money and drugs over the ones he was supposed to love unconditionally. He thought about the woman he decided to make his wife years and years ago. She was the most beautiful woman he had ever laid eyes on. She was the only thing in the world to ever make him feel whole, and the only one that he gave his heart to. He met her when he went to the states. Any other time he wouldn't have paid any attention to a woman of her stature. She was raised in the hood and it showed in her demeanor, but her feistiness intrigued him. She refused to respect him just because he pulled up in a designer suit and a foreign vehicle. She wasn't impressed by the big suitcase of money he brought to the bando. She was the only one never intimidated by his presence. To her, he was just another man with money trying to buy the world. The drug game was nothing new to her, she knew what he was about, and despite his affiliation, she wasn't enthralled. Nor did she fear him, and that fascinated him. Once his business venture was over he *stayed behind, determined to woo her and make her fall in love with him. It didn't happen overnight, and he had to put in major work to just get her attention. However, eventually she did fall in love with him, and she allowed him to sweep her off of her feet. She had nothing going for her there, so it didn't take much to talk her into leaving the country with him afterward.*

They were happy together for years, or so Don thought. After their second child, Don began to see her grow weary of the life that he had made for her. The eyes don't lie, and no matter what he did, it seemed that he could not bring the life back into hers. When traveling on business ventures he would be gone days and sometimes weeks at a time. He and the kids were all she had, and she tried to get him to see that all she wanted was some of his time. Like the time he spared when he was trying to sweep her off of her feet. He understood where she was coming from, yet he still tried to reason with her. His family ran the Dominican Cartel, so when his father died, naturally he had to take over. His family was very powerful and had a reach that wrapped around the world; it was something that he wouldn't be able to give up . . . something that he wasn't willing to give up. That was why he tried to make her a part of it, thinking that would be enough for her. She told him on more than one occasion that he had more than enough money to get out of the game and live a normal life with her and the kids. Yet he would steer her mind away from those thoughts with the lavish gifts he would bestow her with.

Eventually the gifts weren't enough, and the empty promises he gave her fell on deaf ears. She needed more and what he was giving was just material. She thought unconditional love came naturally when it came to family, but it was apparent that their definitions of it weren't matching up. He loved his family with all of his life, but at the end of the day he loved making money more.

The day she left, his heart broke, but knew he would never be able to give her what she needed. Bringing her into this life had been selfish of him. He was a very selfish man. He had wanted her so bad he never thought about the fact that he would never be able to give her 100 percent of himself. She left him a note that he to this day kept in the dresser beside his bed.

Don,
You are my heart. When I met you I swear I could not see past you, but now I see it is only because I didn't want to. I have tried to make this work, even through all of my unhappiness, but I cannot live in a house without love any longer. The money and lavish life mean nothing if I have to fake a smile in my own home. I am taking the kids. They deserve to live a normal life. Don't look for me, and don't worry about us. I have always been able to manage on my own, even before I met you. I love you Don, don't ever forget that. But it is time that I move on. Good-bye.

His family was very knowledgeable and it wasn't long before he found out her whereabouts. Don respected her wishes and kept his distance. He loved them, but his stupidity and his focus on things that shouldn't have come first clouded his judgment. If he could do it all over again he would have picked his family. He was never complete after she left, but he filled her absence with new women and money. Years went by and he had aged with resentment within himself and guilt. He kept tabs on his children but never reached out to have a relation-ship. He thought of everything that he had lost because *of the life that he had chosen to live. The world of money and drugs were the only two things he ever knew, he didn't know how to be happy outside of it. Eventually it took a toll on him, and he realized that he didn't want to live the rest of his life alone, without the love of his life. There were many women who had replaced her spot in his bed, but never in his heart. He took a break from his work and decided to make a trip to the States to find her. To his dismay, he found that he was too late for his love and his children. He learned that the love of his life was dead, and so was his only son. His daughter was so strung out on drugs that there was no saving her. No amount of rehabilitation would help her.*

He couldn't help but to blame himself, as he knew it was his fault. It was punishment for his selfishness. If only he had given her what she needed, she would still be alive. If only he had listened to her pleas for his undivided attention and love, she would have never left. With him, no harm would ever have come to his family. He had not been there to protect them. He had not been there to guide his children. He wasn't there to treat his daughter like a princess, therefore she accepted being treated like a servant at the hands of the drug of her choice. Before he went back to his country with a heavy heart to continue business as usual he decided to stop at Amore, an Italian restaurant that he was familiar with. What he found there was more than good food. There, not only did he regain his hope . . . he was given a second chance.

Chapter 1

They say the hardest things about life are the painful memories, and I have to say that I agree. I remember lying in my own blood on my old bedroom floor, gasping for air. The battle for life or death had complete control of my mind and body as they played a game of tug of war with my soul. I lay beside my grandmother's cold body and was prepared to join her in the afterlife, but still, a part of me wasn't ready to go just yet. However, if it was my time, I refused to repent, because I regretted nothing that I had done in my life. I was just going to accept death as it was. The pain that I felt was unbearable, and I clenched my eyes shut hoping that it would numb itself. The bullet embedded in my stomach made me choke on my own blood, and I was barely able to force air into my lungs.

Khiron and Mocha had left me to die alone cold and in the dark. Khiron, bitter and lost, had single handedly taken everything I'd worked for, loved, and created. I made one mistake, and that mistake was trusting Mocha. Like Ray said, all your niggas ain't loyal. Still, her double cross was one that I wouldn't have seen if it had stared me directly in the face. Just as I began to succumb to my fate I felt a searing pain in my stomach. It felt as if someone was cutting a hole in my body, because that's exactly what was happening. I heard a pleading, distant voice calling my name over and over.

"Stay with me, Say," a hazy voice called from a distance. "Stay with me, mama."

My vision wasn't very clear, but opening my eyes, I was able to make out Adrianna's tear stricken face. Her hands were covered in blood as she set a sharp knife to the side and inserted a straw into the small hole she'd made in my lung.

"It's okay, mama," she whispered in my ear, cradling my head in her arms. "Help is on the way. I'm not going to let you die in here. Just hold on, Say. Hold on."

Something overcame me . . . it felt like relief. I tried to offer up a weak smile, but I don't know if it ever showed on my face, because the next thing I knew I had blacked out.

One month later, I awoke in a hospital bed. My body felt weak and I had tubes connected to it. My throat instinctively made swallowing motions, and it registered to me that I had a tube down my throat too. I used all of the strength that I could muster to pull the uncomfortable thing out and toss it to the side. Devynn was the first person I saw. Her usually curly afro was neatly combed, wrapped in an African hair scarf. She sat up straight, smiling, once she saw that my eyes were open. The smile quickly faded once she heard the first words out of my mouth.

"Where is Ray?" My voice was raspy because it hadn't been used in a while. It was barely audible.

Devynn seemed to stumble over her words, trying to tell me something that just wouldn't come out. She looked at me with eyes full of sadness before finally just shaking her head. I was confused at what was going on around me. I just wanted to see my cousin.

"Adrianna?" Devynn said with a slight plea in her tone.

At that moment I took notice of somebody sitting beside me to my right. My neck was stiff, but I summoned the energy to turn my head to face her.

"Where's Ray?" I asked again. "I want to see him."

Adrianna looked no different, except there was sadness in her eyes. Tears welled in them and slowly began to fall

"He won't be coming, Say," Adrianna didn't sugar coat it. "He's dead."

Suddenly it all hit me like a ton of bricks. I lay there as the past slowly came back to me. I remembered Grandma Rae's dead body, the video, Khiron . . . Mocha. She betrayed me. She turned me, her best friend, in for a man that clearly didn't give a damn about her. He killed my cousin. They both killed my cousin. In a split second, my screams filled the hospital as I cursed the world. I wanted to know why I wasn't allowed to die too. Without Grandma Rae and Ray I had nothing left to live for. I tried to tear out the needles in my body and jump out of bed, but I failed miserably. I was weak, and at that moment death seemed so sweet. I cursed Adrianna and Devynn for saving me and told them they should have just left me in Grandma Rae's house. Yet, the two of them were there with me the entire time. They held me tightly and we all cried on each other's shoulders. When the nurses heard the commotion and told them to leave, they stayed planted by my side. I realized then, in my sorry state, that those two women were all I had left from my previous life. They were my only family. The two of them visited me every day until I was able to start my physical therapy, and even then they were there throughout it all. The next five months consisted of nothing but working hard to get back to my regular physical state and reevaluating my life. I didn't know where I wanted to go from there. I was alive, which is something I was grateful for, but what did I want to do with the rest of my life?

I was flown to Miami as soon as I was stable enough to be moved. Dev and Adrianna didn't want word of my survival to hit the streets. They knew Khiron would be skeptical if a body didn't turn up, so they held a funeral service for me. Except it wasn't me in the casket. It was really the corpse of a nameless prostitute no one would miss. Money talks, and Devynn paid a plastic surgeon to operate on the dead girl's face and make her resemble me as closely as possible. I was dead to my city; the city that had once showed me so much love. The businesses were sold so that Khiron could not profit from them, and ones that had pledged loyalty to The Last Kings were silent. I understood though—with their bosses dead to them, a dollar was only a dollar. Still, it pained me to know what was going on, because Khiron wasn't a boss. He was just a man that lucked up at the right time. He talked like the man, but he didn't move like him. He would never be Ray.

It took a while for her to finally be able to finally speak about it, but Adrianna told me the the gruesome details of Ray's death. No matter what bad Ray did in this world, he did a ton more good, he didn't deserve to die painfully like that. There would have been more honor in him dying by a bullet, but of course Khiron couldn't let him have that. He wanted to demean him. The thought of Ray not being able to have a proper burial due to what the acid had done was almost too much for my heart to bear. Ray had always been my rock and protector; with him gone so was a piece of my soul. My heart was black and a part of me was chipped away. Every day was a work in progress, but I grew stronger with each sunrise. After six months of being in the hospital I was finally allowed to go home, except I didn't have one of those anymore. I ended up moving into the three-bedroom condo Devynn and Adrianna had purchased. The two of them tried to make me feel as comfortable as possible, but it still took a few months after my release to get accustomed to life in Miami. I drove a 2015 red Chevy Cruz, nothing too flashy so that I would not draw attention to myself. We had enough money to sit on for a while, so working was something that we didn't have to do at that point in time.

However, we all were used to a certain type of lifestyle, and those needs wouldn't lay dormant forever. I was a hustler, and although I was a female, I was a king. No matter how I tried to evade it, no other life would suit me. Ever.

I was still trying to get a grip on life as it was, and it didn't help that Devynn and Adrianna had started to act funny around the house. I started to notice how whenever I entered a room, the two of them would cease their conversation abruptly. They also would leave and not inform me on where they were going, nor would they even try to include me. It didn't take long before I grew tired of spending my days by myself. It was sad because I had nobody but them and it seemed like they were shutting me out. The day finally came when I figured it was time to kill the elephant in the room. I walked into the house late one evening, dropped my bags on the floor by the door entrance and shut the door behind me. Walking toward the large living room area I heard a rushed conversation so I decided to stop at the doorway and listen.

"I don't know if Sadie is ready yet, Dev," Adrianna was saying.

"What do you mean, 'ready'?" Devynn spat back. "Yo, it's been like nine months and our funds are running low. I don't know about you, but I'm tired of living like a normal bitch. I'm not going back to a fuckin' nine to five, understand?"

"I know, Dev. Trust me, I do," Adrianna said, her Hispanic accent laying on thick. "I understand, okay? But we are all we have. We already fucked up once, this is no time to rush shit and be hasty. We have to start our foundation again."

There was a silence, and knowing Devyn that meant that she agreed with what Adrianna was saying.

"And with the Italians and Dominicans feuding, we've already picked our side. Once we're on again we're going to be in the middle of a full-fledged war, mama," Adrianna continued. "I've never followed behind a bitch before, but when Vinny gets here Sadie has to be ready to lead. It's what Ray would have wanted."

The respect in her voice when she spoke Ray's name brought tears to my eyes, but that moment was ruined by what I heard next.

"Tyler came by last night," Devynn said. "She was sleep, didn't even know he was here."

My heart pounded. Tyler was here? In Miami? I hadn't seen him since Jamaica. Devynn told me that they had tried to move him to Miami as well, but that he had mysteriously disappeared from the hospital. It didn't surprise me. Tyler was a fighter and staying in that hospital was too dangerous. I figured he'd turn up sooner or later. Not a day went by without him on my mind. I often thought about our last day in Jamaica. The feeling of him inside of me was still so fresh in my memory, and the sound of his voice in my ear telling me that he loved me replayed in my head every night. The fact that he could be that close to me and not speak hurt me in ways that I couldn't even explain. How could he be so intimate with me at one point but not show me any love when I needed it the most? I knew he had to have felt the pain that I did, so how could he just not come to me? Did that night not mean anything to him after all?

"Any news on Marie?" Adrianna asked.

"Nah, that nigga looks restless. He doesn't think Khiron killed her and I agree. Khiron is too messy, that slimy muhfucka would have left her stinking on a corner somewhere. The only thing is, if she is alive, where is he keeping her? Tyler has been everywhere, but you know he has to be low, he's not even supposed to be alive."

My blood was still boiling at the fact that Tyler was so close to me and didn't say one word. Every time Devynn or Adrianna said his name I just got more angry. I'd given myself to him mentally and physically, but in return I couldn't even get a hello? I felt slighted, and all his promises seemed more like lies at that moment. It broke my already broken heart all over again. I'd heard enough. I emerged into the room with a stony expression on my face.

"So this is what you two have been doing behind my back," I shook my head at their guilty expressions.

The two of their heads jerked toward the living room doorway. The shock on their faces was priceless.

"Say—" Adrianna started trying to defend her case, but I silenced her with the palm of my hand.

I glared at the women before me and shook my head again, walking toward the one person sofa across from the couch they were on. Once I was seated I clasped my hands together, not taking my eyes off of them.

"What the hell is going on? And Devynn, you told me you didn't even know where Tyler was when I asked. So you lied to me?" I spoke calmly, trying not to let my anger overcome me as I kicked off my Steve Madden sandals and leaned back into my chair. "Also, why is it that I didn't know about the feud between the Italians and the Dominicans? That sounds like a bit of news that should definitely be in my mental."

"We never meant to keep all of this from you," Adrianna quickly explained, reading my body language like the back of her hand. "You were still recovering, Say. I didn't want to put too much on your plate with all of your wounds. Internal and external."

The fact that she knew I was hurting and thought that making decisions for me was the correct way to go about things made me lose it. All they were doing was hurting me more.

"I don't give a *fuck* what you *thought* Adrianna!" I barked at her. "No moves should be made without me knowing about them, period. We are supposed to be in this together and right now you both have me fucked up! Stop looking at me like I'm just this frail-ass little girl. Am I hurt? Hell, yes, I'm hurt, but that's life. You win some and you lose some. The way this happened is fucked up, and it will always cause an ache in my heart. But I can't stop. You're asking if I'm ready? I'm always ready. And because I'm *ready* you have five minutes to bring me up to speed on everything that has been going on so I can call the next shot. Go."

Adrianna looked slightly taken aback while a smirk snuck its way on Devynn's face. I know I was angry, so my words reflected that and came out a little more forceful than I intended them to. Still, with Ray gone it was time for me to grow up.

"Told you," Devynn said to Adrianna.

Adrianna rolled her eyes and tucked her long hair behind her ears before turning her attention back to my patiently waiting face. Crossing her own legs on the couch, she began painting a picture with her words.

"The Dominicans have done great business with the Italians for years with no problem, but now a war has broken out between them."

"Why?"

"Easy. The Dominicans have been supplying Detroit's new kingpin."

"Khiron," I said, suddenly understanding. "Well, that probably pissed Vinny off."

"Beyond it. He views it as blatant disrespect, and it is something that he cannot ignore. Mainly because although Khiron may have taken down The Last Kings, his name still doesn't have enough clout to reach out to the Dominican Cartel."

"So it had to be the other way around," I concluded for her.

I understood why Vinny felt disrespected. Detroit was his gold mine. Even though Khiron had killed three of our generals he was a peasant on the business side of the dirty money. But even I had to admit that with the Dominicans backing him, touching him would probably be harder than I thought.

"Exactly," Adrianna said. "The Italians made a small fortune off of The Last Kings, and supposedly the Dominicans felt undermined. Don feels as if Vinny was doing bad business by not cutting him into his dealings with Ray."

"And now with Ray out of the picture they can get into cahoots with the new boss of the city," I said as I let the news settle in. I held up my right hand and put my left hand to my head. "Wait . . . I'm lost Adrianna. Why would Don go through all of the trouble and invest? Our work died with Ray. I'm positive no operation in Detroit is pulling in numbers like we were."

"Exactly," Devynn told me as if a light bulb was supposed to appear over my head.

Adrianna saw the look on my face and proceeded to elaborate.

"Detroit was the home to the biggest drug cartel known; *we* did that. Detroit was the heart of it all and remember, Say, kings don't die," Adrianna stared intently in my eyes. "Even with Ray dead Don knew it would be only a matter of time before we retaliated and claimed back what was ours. It's not about money, it's about respect. Don wants to put an end to Vinny's money flow, and he knows by getting in with Khiron it will. The Last Kings' soul is in Detroit . . . we can't start over in another city without causing a war."

It finally clicked.

"This nigga is holding the city hostage?"

Devynn nodded at my revelation.

"It's damn near impossible to touch down without being detected. Khiron, thanks to Don, has the majority of the feds on payroll. Even though his little operation isn't as big as ours; with work in two states and with the Dominicans supplying him, he's on, yo. He's untouchable right now."

"Untouchable?" I nodded my head while rubbing my hands together. "Oh, I'ma touch his ass."

Devynn opened her mouth to speak again, but I shook my head at her. She looked at Adrianna and shrugged her shoulders.

"I've heard all I need to hear. Just to be clear, you both *do* know the seriousness of this situation, right? I hope you are ready for this war, because from the sounds of it, we're already in the middle of it by default," I sighed and shook my head, thinking of Ray. It was time to jump to action. "It wasn't supposed to be like this. My cousin's death won't be in vain, I put that on my life. Tryna hold my city hostage? What kind of shit? Adrianna, contact Vinny and set up a meeting for tomorrow. Dev, tell Tyler that if I don't hear from him in the next twenty-four hours we have a problem."

I bent down and picked up my shoes. There were so many thoughts racing through my head, but before I said anything I needed to talk to the connect. We'd been chilling for far too long. We needed work.

Chapter 2

The very second that Adrianna contacted Vinny I knew that there would be no turning back to the quiet life that I'd been living in Miami. This would be my first time face to face with the notorious Vinny. Under any other circumstances I might have felt honored, but the fact remained that my cousin was dead and Vinny went ghost. I understood that Adrianna and Devynn had history and much respect for the man, but Vinny was currently on my shit list. His money and knowledge stretched far and wide—he was the head of the Italian mafia after all. There was no doubt in my mind that he knew I wasn't dead and I couldn't understand why he didn't reach out and come to me. He did great business with Ray, being that Ray was his protégé. We could have nipped everything in the bud and killed Khiron.

The day of the meeting finally came and early in the afternoon I sat on the queen-sized bed in my room, allowing myself to succumb to my thoughts. Adrianna informed me as soon as I woke up that morning that Vinny would be in Miami at seven o'clock that night. We would meet at the Four Seasons at eight and I was to wait in the lobby for a man with a red tie. As I sat in my room I stared silently at the four walls that boxed me in. I had never felt more lost than I did at that very moment. Before, it had always been easy for me to lead, simply because I was walking in Ray's footsteps. He leveled me and showed me the way of a boss. He was taken away from me too soon, and his teachings weren't finished. I didn't know if I had what it took to lead without him showing me what exactly a leader was. There was no doubt in my mind that I would reclaim that title, but at what cost? Who else would I lose on my journey back to the top? My thoughts were interrupted when I heard three light knocks on my door.

"Come in," I said, just loud enough to be heard, knowing it was Adrianna or Devynn coming to prep me for my meeting.

When the door opened and the person stepped into my room, it felt like my heart stopped beating.

"Tyler," I breathed, taking in the man before me.

His light skin seemed smoother than I remembered, and his hazel eyes seemed darker somehow. The Adidas hoodie with the matching joggers went well with the white and black shell toe Adidas he had on his feet. He still rocked a fade with his curly hair, but he had allowed his facial hair to grow out. His muscular build demanded my eyes' attention. We soaked in each other's appearance for what felt like forever, neither knowing what to say. I told myself that when I saw him I was going to tear into him like an extended clip, but having him in my presence gave me goose bumps, and I remembered our last night in Jamaica. I couldn't muster a word. Our eyes stayed lost in each other until he finally spoke.

"Sadie," he started, and his voice automatically brought tears to my eyes. "I failed you, ma."

He stood in the doorway, not daring to move. He looked at me with such sincerity and I let my tears flow freely. My lip quivered and it didn't take long for him to become a blur.

"This ain't how shit was supposed to be. I know you probably hate me, and I feel that. With Ray gone and Marie missing I had to go solo for a little while. I didn't need the distractions of a relationship throwing me off my game. I know you might not understand, but hopefully you respect it. I just . . . I just had to do shit my way."

I looked at him for a second longer before I wiped the tears from my eyes and face. I cleared my throat and let the soft sarcastic laugh escape my lips.

"I'm assuming this isn't an apology," I whispered, keeping my eyes on my open palms. It seemed to be the only way that I could hold my tears back. "You know, I could go on and on asking you, *'How could you leave me when I needed you the most?'* I could run up and hit you dead in your shit . . . but I'm not, you know why?'

Tyler stood silent.

"Do you know?" I raised my voice.

"Why?" he asked submissively.

"You already said it," I said to my hands. That method wasn't working anymore because I felt more tears drop out of my eyes. "You failed me. The disappointment I feel is so strong. I know to never believe in you again."

Tyler finally made his move for my bed, perhaps to wipe my tears away, but I held up my hand.

"No," I said forcefully.

"Devynn told me you wanted to see me," he told me, still advancing on me.

"Clearly," I said. "And now I've said all I needed to say."

He sat on my bed and pulled me into his broad chest. I tried to push him off of me, but it was no use. Yes, I wanted to fight him off, but I couldn't gather the strength, because I wanted to be in his arms, too. My heart was drawn to him. All I could do was melt into his strong body and let his shirt catch my tears.

"Don't be like that, Say," Tyler said into my soft hair. "You know the game. My nigga is gone. I had to handle it how I knew how to handle it. And real shit, I still haven't gotten a grip on it. I keep expectin' this nigga to hit my line, talkin' about a move we need to make. Or to pull up in the Hummer. My nigga is gone because of the same person that has my baby sister, Say! This shit is killing me."

I was silent listening to his words. From where my head was positioned on his chest I could hear his heart beat accelerating.

"When I found out that you were alive I knew it was best for me to stay away. It wasn't easy to do, because the last thing that I wanted to do was cause you more pain. I knew that your mind would understand but your heart wouldn't. At the end of the day we are both hurting inside, but business must continue. With The Last Kings movement on pause I had to handle some business of my own. If I want to get Marie back my mind has to be clear."

As much as I wanted to be mad at Tyler I just couldn't. I understood everything he was saying, and if the shoe was on the other foot I would have done the same thing. When it was all said and done business came first, our personal feelings for each other would have to wait. My silence spoke volumes as I nodded my head and allowed his strong soft hands to wipe my tears away. I was weak behind Tyler. He was all I had left from the life I lived. I opened my mouth to speak but there was a knock at the door that ended all conversation. Devynn poked her head through the door.

"Um, bruh, Say needs to start getting ready," she said in a dismissive manner.

Tyler kissed my forehead.

"I love you, ma. I'll be in touch," he said in my ear before he stood up from the bed and walked toward the door. "Sleep with one eye open, my nigga," he threatened Devynn in response to her rude tone as he passed her.

Devynn rolled her eyes and stepped out of his way so that he could get out of the door. When he was gone she turned her attention back to me and raised one of her eyebrows.

"You good?"

"Yea," I replied. "Can you run me some bath water please?"

"Um, no bitch. We have no maids around here," Devynn cut her eyes at me.

I rolled mine in response.

"Mocha would do it."

As soon as the words were out of my mouth I realized the error and felt a strong pang of anger and hurt. Devynn noticed the look on my face and instantly her expression softened.

"I still can't believe it was Mo . . ." she let her voice trail.

I couldn't believe it was her either. The person that I thought I knew as well as I knew myself. We had gone through so much together I would never have questioned her loyalty. Ever. Still, my best friend betrayed us all. She let the enemy know where we laid our heads, and that was unforgivable. My blood boiled just at the thought of her, and I couldn't wait to end her life. Because of Mocha, my cousin was dead and I had to assume a position I wasn't ready for. All because she had gotten sprung off of a monster.

"I'm going to kill her," I whispered.

Devynn smiled.

"My nigga," she nodded approvingly. "Cross us once and you won't get a second chance to. Feel me?"

I nodded, getting up from my bed and heading to my closet.

"I'm gon' run this bath for you and make it all bubbly and shit, but don't get used to it. Adrianna said there is an all-black dress with matching studded stilettos in your closet."

"Cool," I said, already locating the Dior dress.

Devynn removed herself from my room, and when I heard the bath water running I smiled.

I sat in the lobby of the Four Seasons alone. Adrianna and Devynn informed me that I was in good hands, but still, they would stay close. My girls were thorough, and I knew that even though I couldn't see them they were probably staring dead at me. I wasn't worried; I had a tool on my thigh and another in my clutch. I wasn't new to the game and I would never again go into another situation blinded. As I waited, I was approached by several men trying to kick game and a group of drunk people asking me if I was Rihanna. I politely told them all to fuck off and continued to wait for my contact. It was five minutes past eight and I was growing impatient.

"Excuse me," I heard a voice behind me say.

I turned my head and my eyes locked with the darkest eyes I had ever seen. Standing before me was a young Italian man with shoulder length black hair. He wore an all black suit with a red tie. He was very handsome in the face, clean shaven, with a skinny build. His face held a naturally pleasant look on it, but I knew looks were very deceiving.

"Pardon my tardiness, Miss Thomas," he smiled at me, flashing his white teeth. "I am Victor. Please come."

He made a motion for me to get up and I obliged. He linked his right arm in my left and walked me through the crowded lobby where the elevators were. Once inside, he pressed the button with the number twenty. I glanced at the number, making a mental note just in case.

"You are a very beautiful woman," Victor smiled once again at me.

"Don't let my looks fool you," I said back to him.

"No worries," he said, patting my arm. "I know all about you. You are ruthless, and that is what makes you beautiful."

I felt a smile creep to my lips just as I heard a light ding as the elevator doors opened. We stepped out together and he led me down a long hallway, passing a few house keepers until we finally made it to our destination.

"One moment," he said as he dug around in his pocket until he found the room keycard. "Ahh, here we are. He is waiting for you."

He opened the door, unlinking his arm from mine, and told me to go through. When I did, I took in the gorgeous suite before me. It was very large with three bedrooms, a living room, and a kitchen. Instead of furniture in the living room there was a jet black rectangle marble table. At the head of the table sat a man who looked very young, but the wrinkles under his eyes and on his forehead let me know that he wasn't. He looked like a man who had seen and done many things in his life. He had smooth, cream colored skin and a sharp jaw bone structure, and although his face held a hard expression he was very easy on the eyes. He too wore an all black suit, but no red tie. His eyes found me, acknowledging my presence. Subtly, he clasped his hands together, and not a second later did everyone sitting at the table clear it. I knew I was in the presence of greatness so I respectfully waited to be asked to take a seat. I didn't need to be told that he was the notorious Vinny, because I felt it. The aura in the air was that of a king. I gave none of the Italian men passing me eye contact. Instead, I focused on Vinny. He gave me a warm, welcoming smile, and that surprised me.

"You have the same look in your eyes as Ray," Vinny spoke in a low, baritone voice. "Please have a seat."

I did as I was told and chose to sit at the other end of the table to directly face him. I thought I saw a look of approval in his eyes at my selection, but I may have been mistaken.

"Sadie—" Vinny started, but something in me knew I had to speak first; so I interrupted him.

"Why?" I asked, cutting straight to the chase.

Vinny looked taken aback by my words, and to be honest, I was too. Adrianna and Devynn had told me all types of gruesome stories about the man in front of me, so I knew what he was capable of. But at that moment I didn't care, I just wanted to understand.

"Why what, Sadie?" he asked.

"I know it was you who had me flown here to Miami. Nobody else has that much reach. I also know that you have your people watching my back. Next time you have somebody trail me tell them not to follow so closely in foreign whips. It's a dead give away."

Vinny's cheek moved, but I wasn't sure if it was a scoff or a smirk.

"With all that being said, it comes down to the fact that you knew I was alive. If you knew I was alive why didn't you come to me? Money is being lost, and now we're in the midst of a war. All I want to know is why?" I gripped my clutch a little tighter in my hand and paused allowing him to speak.

Keeping my composure was getting harder by the second, but I wanted to skip the bullshit small talk and get directly to the point. After some seconds went by Vinny leaned forward in his seat and looked intently into my face.

"You are right when you say I knew of your survival," he started. "I didn't stay away from you because I *wanted* to. That is what you need to understand. Business never stops because of the loss of a king unless he requests it."

His words caught me off guard.

"What do you mean '*unless he requests it?*' Are you trying to tell me that Ray . . .? No. I don't believe you." I shook my head. "And even if he did ask you to not continue business in Detroit, why would you honor it? I thought money was the motive."

Vinny sighed.

"Raymond and I did great business together. He was my business partner and my protégé, and in a way I looked at him like a son. He had instilled inside of him every making of a king. His movement, the one that you stand so proudly for, was single handedly created by him. I was just the connect. He earned my respect in our first meeting together, and that is very rare. The Last Kings was something the common street hustler dreamed of, but Ray? Ray made it a reality."

"So why would he want it to stop?"

"Because of you," he said simply.

"Me?" I asked.

It wasn't clicking in my mind as to why Ray would stop everything because of me. Many thoughts flooded my head, but none of them seemed to connect. Did Ray not feel that I could replace him? Did he think I'd cause the cartel to fail?

"Victor!" Vinny called sharply interrupting my thoughts.

Not five seconds later did Victor appear. He pushed a wooden cabinet over to the table and positioned it in front of me. Vinny pressed a button on the remote Victor handed him before his departure, and the doors to the cabinet opened slowly only to reveal a television behind it.

"What is this?" I asked, looking at Vinny.

"Watch," he instructed and pressed a button.

"With all due respect, I didn't come here to watch a movie. I came here to—" I stopped abruptly when I heard a deep voice come from the television. It was a voice that I could only hope to hear in my dreams now.

"*Sadie,*" I turned my attention back to the television and saw Ray posted on it, looking very much alive. He was sitting on a couch in a living room that I'd never seen before. "*If you're watching this video, that means I'm dead.*"

I stared at the video in disbelief. His dreads were neatly twisted and pulled back. He wore tan cargos and a forest green Ralph Lauren button up. I dropped my clutch on the table and took in my cousin's appearance. I watched his chest go up and down as he inhaled; proof that he had once lived. Clenching my teeth, I tried to stomach the overpowering sadness welling up in my chest.

"*Don't be sad, shorty, and you better not drop not one tear from this video,*" He smiled and I smiled sadly back. "*I love you, Say. You are my heart and I can't do nothin' but hope you never have to watch this video. But shit it is what it is. Live by the game, die by the game. I know you wondering why my man Vinny is showing you this shit in the first place, right?*"

I glanced at Vinny, but his eyes were on the TV. I turned my attention back to my cousin's handsome face.

"*Since the beginning, you've put in mad work; I trust you with everything. You are the rightful heir to everything that I have worked to obtain, Say. You're the only one that I believe can truly hold this shit down. Tyler lacks discipline, and the others still have a lot to learn. Time in the game means nothing when you have the heart of a hustler. All of it comes so naturally to you.*"

"So why would you take it from me?" I asked aloud, to the TV.

"*No matter how you are at the flip, at the end of the day I never wanted this life for you. You were supposed to be a scholar or something. Sometimes I regret putting you on, I feel like I threw you in front of a moving train.*

You are such a beautiful young woman, smart too. You should be in school toting books, not pistols," Ray shook his head. *"With me gone, my crown will automatically go to you, but I would never put that on you without giving you the choice."*

I could barely breathe as I listened to Ray's words. I was beginning to understand.

"I asked Vinny to sever all business and end the whole operation if I was ever clipped. Unless you came directly to him and accepted the position yourself, The Last Kings would be no more. I have a few accounts nobody but Vinny knows about. Combined, there is a little over five million dollars. It's all yours. It's enough for you to live comfortably without having to hustle. You can live a normal life."

It touched me that he had thought that much into depth about the life that he wanted me to live. The only thing was, what he was pitching didn't even sound the least bit appealing. I cocked my head slightly at the TV and made a face. Ray laughed on the TV.

"Well, I guess if you're watching this video that means you've already made your decision, huh? Straighten your face, shorty. You're in charge now, Sadie. Respect is something niggas know nothing about. Make them fear you. Make niggas weary to even speak your name. You're a woman, so these niggas will try you; all I can say is be safe, and think by clicking that finger."

"I know," I said to TV Ray.

"I know you know," he paused, smiling. *"Trust the Italians. Vinny will take you under his wing; you can trust him. He's good people. Take care of the team and always lead, but never be afraid to follow. Your know-it-all ass don't know everything, remember that. Death before dishonor. . . ."*

"Loyalty over all," I finished for him, and he smiled again; like he could hear me.

"That's right. I love you, Sadie. You will never be without me, shorty. Kings don't die. Even in the grave, we live on forever," he kissed his two fingers and gave the peace sign. *"One."*

The video stopped and the room was silent.

"Oh, Ray," I whispered.

I refused to let my tears fall because Ray had told me not to. Instead, I kissed my two fingers and reached to press them on his face, frozen on the TV screen. I took a deep breath and locked eyes with Vinny once more. Swallowing the lump in the back of my throat, I knew it was time to put my size seven foot into Ray's size ten shoe.

"This has gone on for way too long. I will never leave the game until I'm dead. And even then, I want to be buried in a casket on top of twenty bricks and stacks of hundreds," I clasped my hands together and leaned forward, placing my elbows on the table. "The Last Kings is officially back in business. I do believe I have five million dollars and you're the connect, right? Well, I need some work."

Chapter 3

I left the meeting with Vinny feeling whole again. Vinny respected Ray, and by letting The Last Kings fall showed his loyalty. He sacrificed his money flow just so his protégé could rest in peace. Vinny told me that before we could move forward we needed to strengthen our connections and numbers. There were only four of us now, but I knew exactly how I was going to do that.

"Legacy is expecting our call," Vinny told me upon our departure. "He's been waiting for you to reach out. Trust him."

I said my good-byes and allowed the driver to open the door to my limousine. I got in, trying to put all of the moves that needed to be made in order inside of my head. Before I could do that, though, I was ambushed by Adrianna and Devynn.

"That didn't take long."

I looked up to see Adrianna and Devynn chilling in the seats of my Hummer limo; drinks in their hands like they owned the vehicle. I shrugged my shoulders at Devynn's remark.

"Well?" she asked eagerly, and both she and Adrianna stared, awaiting my response.

In the five minutes that presided after Vinny and I parted I'd already formulated a plan. It was time to take charge.

"Put those drinks down," I instructed them and waited until the deed was done to continue. "We are no longer in limbo. Our movement continues tonight. Adrianna, we need a bigger house. The current spot isn't going to work." Adrianna's eyes widened, catching my drift. Devynn sat next to her, smiling like a fat kid in the candy store. "With this shit between the Italians and the Dominicans we obviously can't go home. So instead, we're going to build a new empire here in Miami."

"Say, I don't know if that is a smart idea," Adrianna said skeptically. "Legacy won't take too kindly to another operation running in his city. That nigga is a loose cannon."

I was waiting for one of them to bring Miami's king-pin into it. I smirked at his name. While Devynn and Adrianna were in fact a big part of The Last Kings, some things were still unknown to them. Legacy was the only other boss in existence that I knew of, who could almost hold a candle to Ray. That was why he and Ray did such great business together. Each of Ray's businesses was the drug connect to a different city, and unknown to Devynn, her business was Miami's.

"We need to expand, Adrianna. Right now we only have money and work but no team. There won't be *another* operation in Miami," I smiled at them. "Just one. We have the brains. Legacy has the location."

"How do you know he's going to be good with this shit, Sadie?" Adrianna asked. "And if he's not, then what?"

Adrianna had always been the sensible one, always watching her back and not wanting to step too far out of line. But there were some things that she didn't know. I reflected back on the first time that I had met Legacy. . . .

I was steady as Ray helped me up the steps to the grand ballroom inside of Amore. I was dressed ele-gantly in a strapless, ruby red Vera Wang gown that stopped just above my ankles. My hair was pinned to one side with big, loose curls falling over my shoulder.

The jewelry that I had decided on was simple: a diamond choker around my neck and diamond studs in my ears. Ray stood beside me, looking just as breathtaking. His dreads were twisted back and on his body was a dark, chocolate brown Armani two-button suit. We made our way through the crowded dance floor, commanding all eyes. Ray shook many hands in passing, and I saw his eyes fall on a couple of beautiful women, but none were beautiful enough to make him stop. We made our way to where a very handsome, muscular young man was sitting alone.

"Legacy," Ray grinned at the man once we were within ear shot. "Always on time, I see."

"That's the only way to be when it comes to business I thought?" The man grinned back, standing up and shaking Ray's hand. He then turned to me. "You must be the lovely Sadie I've heard so much about."

I flashed him a dazzling smile. The look in his eyes was genuine but not thirsty like the many other men who had laid eyes on me.

"And you must be the one of our best clients. Nice to finally see the face behind the name," I said.

He smiled again. He was beyond gorgeous. His hair was cut into a low fade bringing out the perfect structure of his face and full lips. Whenever he smiled two deep dimples appeared on each cheek. His face was clean shaven except for the peach fuzz resting respectfully on his chin.

Ray and I sat at the table with Legacy and before the two of them could say a word to each other I butted in.

"What's her name?" I asked Legacy.

"Excuse me?" he asked, thrown off.

"What's her name?" I asked again.

"How do you figure there is a 'her'?" Legacy asked with an intrigued expression.

"Your eyes," I said simply. "They're trained not to wander."

He cocked his eyebrow at me and leaned back in the chair with his arms crossed. It was quite apparent that he was humored by my response.

"Is that right?" he asked, rubbing his peach fuzz. "Observant, I like that. I like that a lot. Her name is Lace. She's an amazing woman."

"Lace?" I repeated, looking at Ray.

The smile he gave me revealed that the connection to the name of his strip club wasn't just a coincidence, and I chuckled.

"She must be a wonderful girl," I concurred, and allowed the meeting to continue.

Legacy was there to complete a business deal with The Last Kings and to personally restock. Business was going great as usual, and I just sat there and listened to two great men work. I had no clue why Ray had asked me to come along to the meeting; I could have been counting stacks in the money room. Nothing special happened in the meeting, and upon parting the two men slapped hands in farewell. I was positive that I saw a little white paper go from Ray's hand to Legacy's, telling him where to pick up I was sure.

"It was a pleasure meeting you, Sadie," Legacy said to me, and he bent down to kiss my hand. "I look forward to doing business with you in the future."

I snapped back to reality and looked at Adrianna and Devynn's faces. At the time, I didn't take in Legacy's words, but now, thinking back to that night, I knew there was a deeper meaning. I nodded my head at Adrianna.

"There is no doubt in my mind," I said. "I'm offering him a seat at a table full of kings forever. All I'm asking for in return is to borrow his city for a few months, just until we're completely equipped to go to war. Adrianna?

I'm going to need my down-ass bitch to return, I don't like all of the second guessing that you have been doing."

I knew my words caught her off guard, but I had to let her know I wasn't feeling her new attitude. Her heart matched mine, and so did her love for the game, but it seemed that lately she was trying to make a change. Fuck that.

"Any decision I make I need you to be down to go. When I tell you to do something I need you to do it. That question you asked has me questioning if you trust me or not. You two are like my sisters, and at the end of the day we are all we have. I trust you, and all I am asking is for the same in return. I'm back, and it's time for us to make these moves again. As a team," I finished.

A look of sadness came over Adrianna's face.

"You sound just like him," she shook her head. "But you're right, and you got it, *Boss*."

"Good," I said looking her square in the eyes. I knew I was different; only a shadow of the old Sadie existed. I motioned toward the glasses they'd set down and poured up my own shot of Hennessy. "Pick up your glasses. Let's toast to a new beginning."

They grabbed their glasses and held them in the air very much like the first official Last Kings meeting at Ray's house some time ago. The only difference was that we were missing four faces.

"For D, Amman, and Ray," I said. "May they rest like kings. Their legacy will live on through us. I would say some more heart felt and sentimental stuff, but this isn't a movie. Niggas will test us because we fell, and now to them we are on the same level as they are. It's time to show the world that kings live forever. We can't *make* these niggas respect us, so instead we'll make them fear us. Never mind the fact that we're females, we have trigger fingers just like the rest of them. No intimidation and no more loss; to a new beginning!"

"The Last Kings," Devynn and Adrianna said in unison.

We all downed our drinks at the same time, and I felt solace knowing that we'd been given the opportunity of a fresh start. It was my time, and I planned on making my way back to the top. In a sense, karma had bit me hard because Khiron and I had switched places. It was me this time, climbing my way back up to the top, trying to stake my claim on what was rightfully mine. The only difference was that when my bullets entered his body I would make sure that he was dead.

Chapter 4

"Noooooo! Please. Please, I will do anything you want. Just don't hurt me anymore."

The sounds of a man's spine-tingling, screaming sobs echoed in a theatre full of empty seats. The screams were followed by loud thuds that quieted the annoying noise. Legacy sat watching, emotionless as three of his soldiers tortured a man on the stage before him. He was front row and center in an audience of emptiness, sickly enjoying the show. The man being tortured was known to Legacy as David Jackson. A man that had crossed him in the worst way, and for that, he had to suffer. Legacy met David by chance when he came in with a string of new young and hopeful runners. Legacy wasn't the typical kingpin. Just because you *could* push his work didn't mean that he would let you. He was very weary of who he let in his circle for the simple fact that in his position at the top, he was always a target. However after proving himself to Legacy when he took a bullet for him, Legacy opened the doors to his underground operation to David. Legacy welcomed David to the world of his cartel off of the strength that he made the mistake of thinking David was thorough. He was sadly mistaken. A few months after being welcomed, David moved up in the ranks gaining more and more of Legacy's trust. Things went completely downhill when Legacy put him on the same level as his most loyal and told him the location of his main drug house.

Ghost, Legacy's best shooter, had always felt an uneasy vibe whenever David was around. There was just something about his eyes and the way they looked at everything . . . almost like they were looking for something to tell on. His suspicions were soon proved right after a drug bust gone wrong. It came to light then that David was an undercover detective sent to infiltrate Legacy's illegal dealings and put him away for life. However, the day of the bust, something told Ghost to tell Legacy to move all of the product and drug money from that trap. Listening to his boy and moving the work might have proven to be the best decision Legacy ever made in life, because when the feds kicked down the door they found nothing but an old dopehead couple lying high as a kite on a dirty mattress.

After that incident there was no way that Legacy could let David live. For one, he knew too much, and for two, he had committed the ultimate crime. He would be judged in the streets. When Legacy was done with him, no part of his body would be recognizable. Family and friends of David thought he was away in New York in protective custody, but really he was twenty minutes away from his home, dying a slow and painful death. On the stage there was already a beautiful mural painted with blood, and David was already missing all of the fingers on his right hand.

"Do you know what happens," Legacy's deep voice spoke softly from his seat, "to snitches? Or maybe they didn't teach you that at the academy."

"Please, man," David said, shaking violently in the chair he was bound to. His body was going into shock. "My wife is pregnant! I was just doing my job."

"A job that would have taken my life," Legacy chuckled. "What makes yours better than mine? Here I am thinking that God made us all equal. You've seen firsthand what

I've done to people who have done wrong by me . . . but you? You *really* thought that shiny badge would protect you."

"Please," David's eyes expelled more tears.

"Shut up!" Legacy shouted and his voice echoed menacingly throughout the theatre. "What I do has nothing to do with you, it affects your life in no way. Still, you had to go *out* of your way to try and put me in a hole. For what . . . the glory? A fifteen-minute slot in the ten o'clock news."

David blinked away the tears in his eyes frantically at the accusations Legacy was making. He was quiet, mainly because they were true. He had in fact seen Legacy commit murder firsthand. He had also seen how those under Legacy coward at his feet. Still, the thought of being Miami's hero for bringing down its biggest threat on guns and drugs was enough for him to keep going. He never thought that he would get caught up, especially since he was so sure that his fellow detectives would run up in a house full of money and dope. Once it got back to him that it all had been moved, he knew that he was outed. The chief of the precinct set it up so that he would safely be sent away to New York until things settled down at home. His pregnant wife and children were to soon follow, however he never even made it on the plane. His whole right arm had gone numb from the pain of losing all of his fingers, and at that point he knew there was no chance for his survival. He had committed treason by crossing Miami's kingpin. The biggest mistake that he made was believing that he was untouchable because he was protected by the law. He hadn't yet learned that money spoke volumes, and for the right price, you were above the law. It was too late for him.

"I'm tired of hearing this nigga beg. Cut his tongue out," Legacy instructed Ghost.

The tears streaming down David's face didn't move Legacy at all. Simply because he was crying over his own life, a life that held no value to Legacy. Just as Ghost had the scissors opened on David's tongue and prepared to make one swift snip, Legacy's phone vibrated violently in the pocket of his gray 501 Levis. He held his hand up, signaling for his men to pause.

"Hello?" he said into the phone after he pressed it to his ear.

"Noon tomorrow," a woman with a Hispanic accent said on the other end. "The address is in the armrest of your Mercedes. Beautiful car, by the way, but wrong color."

Legacy chuckled, not needing to know who it was; he'd heard her voice before. It was one he'd once done business with quite often. He was wondering how long it would take for them to make contact.

"She ready?" Legacy asked.

"Beyond," the voice replied. "Don't forget to clean up your little mess. I'll be seeing you."

When the call disconnected he smiled to himself. The Last Kings were still on their P's and Q's. Turning his attention back to the stage his smile quickly faded and he waved his hand.

"Continue," he directed, and welcomed the screams like music to his ears.

The address written in pretty handwriting on the piece of paper led Legacy to a large, beautiful beach house the next day. Legacy was a man who had always admired nice property and upkeep. As a kid he would ride his bike through the nice neighborhoods and scope out all of the houses, hoping to one day be the proud owner of one of them. He had to admit he was impressed by the setup of the home he had just pulled in front of, and he made sure to scope out his surroundings. The house was white with three levels and had a private driveway with on-site parking for four cars. The house was pushed back from the rest of the homes in the neighborhood and was the only one that was that close to the beach. Legacy parked and stepped out of his tan Mercedes, admiring the view of the ocean as he made his way to the tall front door.

"If this is what it's like to 'fall off' I need to fall off more often," Legacy said under his breath and reached to press the doorbell.

Before his finger could even cause a sound to be made inside the house, the door opened and before him stood a very attractive Latina woman. She wore a yellow sundress and let her long brunette hair flow in loose curls over her shoulders. She looked at the diamond studded watch on her wrist and then back at him.

"Eleven fifty, you're early," she said, placing her hand on her hip.

"That's on time, right?" He responded with a warm smile.

"I'm Adrianna," she said returning his smile. "We're out back."

She motioned for him to follow her as she led him through the house. The two of them walked on the hardwood floor and through the main living room area toward a long glass sliding door. The only sound heard was the clicking of Adrianna's heels on the floor and the waves of the ocean smacking against the shore.

"After you," she told him and stepped aside so that he could go through the already open sliding door.

He went around her and stepped on the concrete base of the open balcony. The view of the water was breathtaking, and a little ways away in the sand, a table was set up under a canopy. At the table he recognized one of the faces, although partly covered by an elegant hat, as Sadie.

The other girl had smooth cocoa brown skin and wore a natural curly afro. Not wasting any time, Legacy made his way through the sand in his tan cargos and He Got Game retro 13's until he reached the round table. He sat down under the canopy in an open seat and was thankful that he was shielded from the scorching sun. Adrianna appeared at the table, heels in one hand, and grabbed the brown-skinned girl's arm with the other.

"Devynn, we have some business to handle, don't we?" Adrianna hinted to her.

Without hesitation, the woman named Devynn stood up from the table. Her eyes met Legacy's for a split second, and there was no doubt in his mind that he was looking into those of a cold blooded killer. He nodded his head in respect and watched the two as they went back into the house. When they were gone, Legacy turned his attention back to Sadie, studying her tense face. He remembered when he first met her; she had been one of the most vibrant women he had ever seen. Her long hair blew in the comforting breeze and her face had a calmness about it. Not much had changed about her since their first meeting. Their eyes found each other and that was when he finally saw the difference. Her eyes once held so much happiness and promise. Now they were colder than the Arctic.

"You came alone?" she asked him, raising her eyebrow and breaking the ice.

"I trust you," Legacy smiled at her. "But not that much. I don't go anywhere alone."

Sadie smirked before turning her head slightly to the right. Her eyes naturally fell upon a boat that was quite a ways out. To the untaught eye it simply looked like a couple of people fishing casually, but Sadie knew better. The water was too shallow where they were at, and Sadie was positive that they weren't even fishing at all. The position they were in and the range they had intrigued her.

"Their guns will reach this far?" she asked, using a finger to motion toward the boat.

She had spotted his shooters right off the bat, and Legacy raised his eyebrows at how keen her senses were.

"I almost forgot who I was dealing with. Ray wouldn't have left his empire to a fool," Legacy said, apparently impressed.

"I would offer you a drink," Sadie started crossing her legs and clasping her hands together, "but we can drink later. I'm sure you're wondering why I asked to meet with you today. Do you remember the night we met?"

"Of course," Legacy replied.

Sadie eyed him for a moment. He was just as handsome as he was the last time they'd met. She loved how soft his hair looked, his caramel skin, and the fact that his muscular frame made it seem that he could rescue any damsel in distress. The cunning smile on his face made her trust him, even though she knew he was capable of murder. Savage murder. She cocked her head at him and gave him a knowing look.

"You didn't meet with Ray to re-up. I didn't realize until not too long ago that you had placed an order with Adrianna and received it a week before you touched down. She confirmed it. That piece of paper Ray slipped you didn't have a pick up time and spot on it, did it? What was really on that paper, Legacy?"

Legacy didn't respond right away. He knew then that she was for sure kin to Ray. He stared at her hard expression and felt the respect drench from him to her. Nobody else would dare come at him and speak to him the way she did. Her persistence showed her boss status. She didn't fear him, because to her she was above him. He remembered the last conversation he had with Ray. It was a few days before the double funeral of two of Ray's soldiers. He asked Legacy to keep an eye and an ear out for whoever was bringing war to his city. He also said something else that Legacy didn't pay attention to, thinking that no one would ever catch Ray slipping.

"*Every hustler will have his day. Mine might be sooner than later fam. I chose this life it didn't choose me.*" Ray said on the private jet.

"*Bruh, you tripping. You gon' find that nigga and dead him no doubt,*" Legacy waved his words off, but Ray continued.

"*I brought Sadie with me that night for a reason. One day she will come to you, with or without me. She's all about business. Always looking to expand The Last Kings. Whatever she asks, do it.*"

Legacy came back to reality only to see Sadie's focused expression as she awaited his answer.

"You're right," he said truthfully. "I wasn't in Detroit that night to re-up."

"Then why?" Sadie asked.

"I was there to personally meet the connect," Legacy told her. "Ray wasn't stupid. He knew he wouldn't rule forever. He set it up so that if ever need be I would be able to cop directly. Of course I did business through The Last Kings until shit hit the fan, but I needed work."

Sadie nodded her head like she was finally realizing something.

"Ray must have trusted you," Sadie spoke softly, the hard expression gone from her face. "He didn't want this life for me. He set you up with Vinny as a precaution, just in case I decided to give it all up. He was looking out for you. My cousin was loyal to you, so you must have been loyal back."

Legacy heard the respect in her tone.

"So what type of proposition are you trying to give me?"

"It's simple as this. The Last Kings is down to four. Three technically, since Tyler's sister is missing. He's been on his lone wolf shit. I need a team and I need your city."

Sadie made it seem like she was asking Legacy for a box of Girl Scout cookies, but he didn't know how willing he was to share. He placed a thoughtful hand on his chin and weighed his options. He thought back to Ray's words and knew almost immediately what the answer was. Still, he wanted to know what was in it for him.

"What will I be getting in return?" Legacy asked.

"You will have a place at a table with kings for the rest of your life; even when I'm done using this location. I am positive you know everything that is going on currently. War is breaking out and I want to be prepared for it. I have to be in order to regain control over my city. Detroit is the heart of The Last Kings. I have to for Ray."

Legacy was lost in Sadie's dark eyes. The look in them was sincere. He knew of Sadie's credibility and he also knew she would turn Miami into a gold mine. But stepping down from an empire that you built, temporarily or not, wasn't easy for any man. Still. . . .

"A'ight, shawty. You can take however long you need. Let's just get this money together."

Sadie's lips turned up into a smile before she reached her hand over the table for a handshake.

"Legacy, I'd like to officially welcome you to The Last Kings."

Chapter 5

Holding true to his word, Legacy opened the pearly gates of his operation for us to walk through. With the money that Ray left me I was able to purchase everything I needed from Vinny without being fronted. Legacy matched me on every dime I spent, making him a shareholder in my operation. I put him up on everything that had transpired up until now and also on everything Ray had taught me. Legacy ended all street dealings, and anybody moving that way was considered dirty. In order to wash my filthy money, I purchased a one story vacant building. On top was a hair salon called Diamond Dreams, but in the lower level was the one and only trap. Devynn, the Hair Guru, held down the salon effortlessly. She not only made sure that the under-the-table business ran smoothly, but also that everyone who came in left looking like a star. I sent Adrianna on a business trip to Baltimore, and Legacy sent an array of his own men with her to keep her safe. Before I came into the picture Miami only did business in Miami. It was time to expand and form important alliances. By doing my research, I found out that Baltimore was home to a man cycling dirt throughout his city. That could only be because he had a shitty connect, one that didn't value the comeback of a dollar. Finally, after feeling the man, Row, out I decided that it would be good for The Last Kings to set up shop there. Adrianna put him up on game on how The Last Kings did business. Out with the old, in with the new, and just like that, we were his connect.

My mind was constantly going. Every hour a new way to make money would enter my head. I pitched all of my ideas to Legacy and he never doubted me once. It felt good to sit and talk with somebody who understood the vision. It had been a while since I talked to somebody with a like mind who didn't look at me like a frail, broken woman. When I was alone I kept myself busy with business dealings to keep Ray and Tyler off of my mind. It never worked, though. They always seemed to find a way there. When I thought of Ray it was almost impossible for me to believe that he was truly dead and gone. His voice was still so fresh in my head. When it came to Tyler . . . no matter how much I tried not to care I knew I did. What I really felt was nothing but love for that man, and I wished he would stop being so distant with me. The most I got was a phone call telling me that he was okay, but not saying anything about his quest to find his sister. He wouldn't even let me help, he just told me to focus on my own business. It broke my heart the way he had pushed me away, but I knew I had to let him find his own way back to me.

Business in Miami was slower paced than it was in Detroit. In order to try to pull in the same numbers we had to work twice as hard. The money was racking up quite nicely, however we still weren't seeing the numbers that we were used to. One evening Legacy and I sat on chairs in the sand in my backyard staring at the ocean water. We tried to meet at least once a week to discuss business, and instead of doing so in the dreariness of an office we opted for something more relaxing. The sun was blazing, but the wind mixed with the mist from the ocean cooled our bodies. The sound of the waves crashing into the sand was somewhat soothing, and the view all together was breathtaking. It was the perfect place to kick back.

"I used to say I'd get out of the game once I reached my first million," he told me.

"Well, what happened?" I asked him.

"I spent that shit and had to make another," Legacy said simply. "The game never got out of me. I didn't come from money, but now that I'm use to it I couldn't give this life up if I wanted to."

"I understand. It's like it's embedded in your DNA," I agreed.

I felt that there was something else that he wanted to say, but I didn't press him. I was patient, and sure enough he popped the question I'd been waiting for.

"When are you going to go back to Detroit? You bury yourself in work," Legacy continued. "Even if there is nothing to do you are always trying to keep yourself busy. It's obvious that you're trying to kick something out of your mind. You still hurting, ma. I understand that. But hiding inside of yourself ain't gon' change the fact that Mocha turned on you, and it's not gon' get your city back."

His words stung. It was like he was holding a mirror to my face and forcing me to face every thought I had locked away. I had so many things gnawing at my mental that I hadn't taken the time to sit down and figure out if I was even okay. I was constantly on go mode and making sure that everything else was in place. I stared at Legacy, a little shocked at his observations. He'd become like a big brother to me, but the past two weeks doing business with him had become hard. He was beginning to remind me so much of Ray, and I didn't know if that was a good thing or a bad thing.

"This is something," I started hearing the coldness dripping from my tone. "This is something that you will never understand. So please don't go Dr. Phil on me please nigga. I don't need it. Your best friend didn't betray you. You didn't lose everything you built in a day! Your cousin isn't dead. The work Miami sees in a week? I saw that shit in a day nigga! So don't tell me you understand."

"That's crazy to me," Legacy scoffed, shaking his head, clearly unmoved by my revelation.

"What is?" I asked with my nose turned up.

"That you still feel like you're the only one that felt that loss," Legacy's low bark startled me. "Or think you're the only one who has felt loss, period. You think you're the only one that's hurt? Nah, but listen to me when I say this. Be mad if you want, but I don't give a fuck. That's what happens in the game. How many souls have you snatched? How do you think their families feel?"

I was silent.

"You don't think about it, do you? You just eat that shit and keep it pushing. Now it's your move, so what? Are you going to forfeit because somebody touched your feelings? It's okay to feel pain shorty, but don't ever let pain get in the way of what you know needs to be done. You're doubting yourself and I can tell. Now you tell me, is that what G's do?"

"No," I answered with my eyes on the waves.

"Hell, no. In my last conversation with Ray he said one day you would come to me. And to give you whatever you needed," Legacy's tone softened. "At first I couldn't see myself bowing to a woman, someone younger than me at that. But I know now that I made the right decision. You have the heart of a hustler. In two months your ideas have doubled what I was pulling in before you came. I'd be a fool not to accept the fact that some things are just more important than a position of power. Miami will always be my city, but I'm only one part of the operation. Once The Last Kings is back you will be the king of it all. So what do you need, boss?"

Legacy's words touched me in a place that I didn't know still had emotion. I bit it back and nodded my head.

He was right, it was time to make an official come back. I took a deep breath and focused my sights on the setting sun.

"There is only one operation now," I said swallowing my tears. "This is all The Last Kings, we work together. I don't want there ever to be a struggle of power as long as we understand each other's positions. The respect level will always be in sync. However . . . there is only one thing missing."

"What's good?"

"I need a team," our eyes met again and I saw the smile in his before he even spoke.

"Already done."

After our talk on the beach he held a meeting the next day at his recently purchased home. It was in a beautiful neighborhood called Coconut Grove. His house was much larger than those around it, and the whole perimeter was gated with shooters on guard. After they let me through I pulled my new and freshly washed black on black Chevy Camaro around the circular driveway and parked. Devynn and Adrianna pulled up right beside me in Devynn's red Dodge Challenger. As soon as I opened my car door I saw a beautiful woman with long hair that held wet curls walking toward me. Her brown skin was almost golden in the Miami sun. She wore jean high waist shorts and a turquoise blue crop top showing off her small waist and abs. She had a small nose, slanted eyes, and high cheekbones. Her walk was confident and not at all unsure.

I exited my vehicle, dressed comfortably in a simple off-the-shoulder white sundress with a tan fedora over the two Cherokee braids that I rocked in my hair. The Manolo Blahnik sandals on my feet matched the hat on my head perfectly and the Mink Revlon lipstick on my lips completed my whole look. I could tell that just like I had sized her up, she was doing the exact same thing to me. Not afraid, I walked toward her with my clutch under my left arm.

"You must be Lace," I said knowingly, offering a kind smile.

"And you're Sadie," she replied, her voice bitter sweet. Needless to say, she did not return my smile. "Funny, I thought you would look . . . different."

I paused, not liking how her voice dropped at the word "different." It was at that moment I took notice of the look on her face. It wasn't that of a welcoming housewife. She was not coming off at all like how Legacy had described her, and she was turning me off with every second going by.

"Oh, really?" I asked, looking into her eyes. "What were you expecting exactly?"

"The way Ray and Legacy talked about you, I guess I expected more," she tried me, eyeing our vehicles.

I automatically knew what she meant as I felt Devynn and Adrianna approach us.

"Don't let the exterior fool you. Understand that every material thing is disposable," I told her simply. "I thought the role of the wifey was to make guests feel comfortable. You just lost major points with the person you're supposed to be impressing. Excuse me, Lace McCoy."

I knew Legacy sent her outside to lead us inside, but honestly I was tired of looking at her. I walked around Lace without even introducing her to Adrianna or Devynn and made my way to the door. Adrianna and Devynn followed close behind me toward the already open double doors. Once inside, the cold air and wonderful aroma in the air hit me at the same time.

"The dining room is this way," Lace said, coming from behind us.

Devynn gave me a knowing look, and the look I gave her back was telling her to stand down. Devynn was the type to smack a bitch real quick for disrespect, but I was giving her a pass just because she was Legacy's girl. But one pass was all that she would get. I knew my girls weren't feeling the chick and I wasn't either, but we were there on business. I walked side by side with Lace through Legacy's huge home until we reached the dining room. Sitting at the round table awaiting our arrival were Legacy and two muscular men that I had never seen before. I made sure to make eye contact with them all before Legacy asked us to sit down.

"I believe we all know why we're here," Legacy started once everyone was seated. His eyes circled the table before he continued. "Sadie, that's Ghost," he pointed to the light-skinned man that sat on the right of Devynn. "And this is my right hand, Smoke."

On his right was a chocolate man with a brush cut that had waves so deep they rivaled the Atlantic Ocean, you could dive in. Both men nodded their heads and grunted.

Strike two, I thought to myself because Lace's attitude had been strike one.

"And I think you've already met Lace," Legacy said to me, and I barely looked her way to acknowledge her.

That didn't go unnoticed by Legacy and he raised an eyebrow at Lace who sat on his left. She responded with a shrug. Next to Lace, Adrianna shook her head, and on my right, Devynn gave a low laugh.

Strike three.

"I'm Devynn," Devynn introduced herself. "I would tell y'all my favorite hobby, color, and all that, but I'm sure you don't give a fuck."

I placed my hands together and smirked at my clutch on the table.

"I'm Adrianna," Adrianna said in her sweet voice.

I sighed before I placed my hands down on the table. I knew all eyes were on me and I lifted my head to meet their gazes.

"This," I started, "is supposed to be a table of kings. Not potentials."

I cut my eyes at the new comers. Legacy crossed his arms and leaned back into his chair, allowing me to take the reins.

"What I want to know is why did Legacy just introduce you all to me? What . . . you niggas can't speak? A king always makes *himself* known. How am I supposed to trust you on my team if you can't even think for yourselves?"

"With all due respect," Lace spoke up quickly, glaring at me. "You already dropped the ball in your own city, so how are we supposed to trust *you*? Didn't your best friend betray you for some dick? And isn't the man she threw you under the bus for the same nigga that killed Ra—"

My gun barked before she even had a chance to finish her statement. Out of respect for Legacy I didn't kill her, but for speaking my cousin's name I did cause her pain. Before anyone had a chance to react, blood was splattering from her arm when my bullet connected.

"Ahh!" she cried out and tried to stand up, her left hand flying to her right arm.

"Sit down, bitch!" I said coldly. "Or I'll double that shit."

Ghost and Smoke tried to grab their waists, but Devynn and Adrianna's guns had already claimed their targets.

"Don't try it," Devynn warned, cocking her gun at Ghost's head.

"Legacy!" Lace looked at him, but he just shook his head and handed her a towel from the kitchen.

She stared at him in disbelief, but took the towel. She sat there bleeding, in pain, and Smoke looked at me like I was crazy. His eyes shifted from me, to Legacy, then back to me.

"Legacy is thinking the same thing as me, Lace. You're talking too fucking much. That's going to stop today. You knew who you were meeting with, and you know why. So that little speech was irrelevant. This *was* your city, but as long as I'm here, it's mine. In two months, these two women and I have brought in more money than you have seen by yourselves in six. Because of us, you have no worries. You owe us."

I spoke and I felt the power in my words.

Make them fear you.

Ray's voice popped up in my head, and now I understood them. Fear was another sign of respect, and I needed them to know I was about my money and to never cross me. Ghost and Smoke both still had guns pointed to their heads, but they seemed in a trance listening to me speak.

"I need your help to get my city back. Once that happens I will be out of your hair and peacefully sitting on my own throne."

"You're asking us to go up against the Dominicans?" Ghost's deep baritone voice entered my ears.

"You scared?" Devynn said with her gun still pointed at him.

"I wouldn't be sitting here if I was scared, but only a dumb muhfucka would believe we could go at that nigga with the Dominicans backing him.

"Then I guess you can call us some dumb mothafuckas then, sweetheart," Devynn said.

There was silence for a moment, and for a split second I thought that maybe the meeting had been a dud.

"A'ight," Smoke spoke up from beside Legacy. "I'm down. What's the plan?"

All eyes turned to him in shock and he laughed.

"Aye man, she just shot the kingpin's bitch in front of the nigga. She checks out to me."

"A'ight," Ghost said shrugging his shoulders. "This won't be the first suicide mission a nigga has partaken in."

I smiled and looked to Lace.

"What about you?" I asked, ignoring her bleeding arm and grimacing face. "Are you done running your mouth?"

The hate in her eyes for me was so real and I loved it. She was eating the pain in her arm, and for that she gained an ounce of my respect back. She nodded her head as her answer.

"I thought so. I need you all to trust me. We have powerful allies on our side. No fear, only loyalty. Welcome, put your guns in the air."

Devynn and Adrianna ceased their aim and put their guns up. I loved how defensive they were for me. Hopefully the others would grow to show me such loyalty. A part of me knew I could trust them, though. Legacy had chosen them. Everybody raised their guns until the barrels touched; Lace used her left hand.

"The Last Kings," I said and connected eyes with them all.

"The Last Kings," they said in unison.

Legacy lowered his gun and looked approvingly at me. He called his housekeeper in the dining room and made arrangements for Lace to go to the hospital. Theresa, his housekeeper, didn't even look shocked to see the bullet wound.

"Now you niggas have to get inked up and branded!" Devynn was saying and showing them her tattoo when I felt my phone vibrate.

"Hello?" I said into the mouth piece once I saw who it was.

"I found her."

Chapter 6

Back in Detroit

Mocha's soft moans filled the air as her clit was devoured and her sticky thighs were gripped.

"Khiron!" She cried into the darkness while his tongue circled faster and faster. "Ahh! Baby, you *know* that's how I like it. You're so *nastyyy*."

Her orgasm came full force and she pushed his head further into her love box so he could drink up all of her sweet juices. While her body was still shaking he began to lay sensual kisses on her, from her stomach to her neck until he was at a perfect angle to slip inside of her. He forced himself inside of her without a warning, and her pussy lips automatically clenched tightly around his thick shaft.

"Fuuuuuuck!" Mocha moaned while Khiron sexed her deeply and slowly. She felt the head of his dick thumping against her G-Spot.

"I love you, ma," he whispered. "You love me?"

"Yes," Mocha whispered as her hands scratched up his back and her neck arched. "I love you, baby."

Khiron's hands gripped Mocha's plump ass underneath her on the bed. While he was fucking her into ecstasy, he parted her cheeks and entered two of his fingers into her asshole and held them there. Mocha creamed immediately.

"I love you, Khiron. I love you, Khiron. I—"

Beep! Beep! Beep!

Mocha opened her eyes and looked at the source of the disrespectful noise. The digital clock read ten thirty p.m. Between her legs she felt an uncomfortable moisture and knew she'd had an orgasm in her sleep again. The dream she'd just had wasn't just a dream. It was a memory. A memory of the first time Khiron had ever told her that he loved her. She missed the man she had thought he was. But looking around her tiny bedroom, inside her cramped, one-story house, she wondered if he had ever really existed. She felt disgusted for even having that dream. She and Khiron did still have sex, however it was more of him taking than her actually giving. He was rough with her, and he definitely didn't tell her that he loved her anymore. He didn't care if she was dry or not, he would still take it. It was his way of letting her know she was his property.

Mocha's displeasure of him went beyond measure. She shuddered and threw the covers off of her exposing her thick, mocha colored thighs. She swung her legs over the side of her queen sized-bed and went to the bathroom in her room. Once there, she turned on the shower head and stripped free of her wet shorts and cream cami top. The hot water soothed her body the instant she stepped in. She stood there for a moment and allowed the water to slap against her before she broke down. Gripping her hair, she allowed herself to slide down in the tub and sobbed. Crying had become a part of her daily routine because it was the only way that she could let out her frustrations. Her sins and betrayal followed her everywhere she went. Her best friend Sadie's face invaded her thoughts daily, and guilt overwhelmed her. Although Mocha wasn't the one who had pulled the trigger that ended Sadie's life, her blood was just as much on her hands as it was Khiron's.

She had allowed his promises and lies to consume her to the point where she had turned on her only family. Even after he got what he wanted, Khiron just couldn't get over the fact that Mocha had been in allegiance with the ones that killed his father. He wanted her to feel as if she had nothing and nobody. He downgraded her from a Range Rover to an Impala and moved her to a tiny house in the hood. He allowed her to keep her Last Kings tattoo because she was his living and breathing trophy piece, showing that he'd brought down the best.

"I'm sorry, Say," she sobbed, letting go of her hair and covering her face with her wet hands. "It wasn't supposed to be like this. I miss you so much."

It had been a year, but things never seemed to get any easier. Mocha let the water run all over her hair and face until she finally was able to stand up and wash herself. When she got out, she wiped her eyes before drying her body. Once she saw what time it was she hurried up so that she could get ready for her date that night. By date she meant client. She only set up her dates when she knew Khiron would be gone on business. She usually only met with them on the high end part of Detroit where she knew none of Khiron's thugs would be lurking. That night she would only be making two thousand dollars, which was nothing compared to the two hundred thousand she made daily as a Last King. She would take it, though, because she had no other source of income.

Mocha knew she had the body of a goddess and could get whatever she wanted out of a man. At first selling her body was out of the question, but when she thought about it she knew it was the only way she could secretly stack up without Khiron finding out about it. He refused to let her get a job, so she started one of her own. She met her first client at the doctor's office when she had gone in for her yearly pap smear exam. The way Dr. Howard looked at her, she knew he wanted her. Married and all, she saw the thirst in his eyes as he fumbled with the speculum. After the uncomfortable exam, Mocha didn't wait for the doctor to leave the room to get dressed. She stood up and watched the doctor's eyes widen as she walked over to where her panties and leggings were. She slowly put them on, purposely facing the opposite direction so that he had the perfect view of her round cheeks.

"I-I'll be right back with your discharge papers," he stammered. His white face was now beet red.

"Tell me, Dr. Howard," Mocha said after putting her red heels back on. She walked over to him and used one finger to gently push him down into a chair behind him. "Does your wife give you enough attention at home? Because the way you're eyeing my body is telling me that something is missing."

"I don't know what you mean." Dr. Howard tried to play dumb and swallowed hard.

Mocha chuckled. Putting her hands on his shoulders, she bent down until her cherry red lips were right by his ear.

"You want to fuck me, don't you?" she purred into his ear. "Hard? Soft? Fast . . . or slow?"

She removed her right hand from his shoulder and placed it between his legs. She was surprised at the older man's size as she felt it awaken from her touch. She let out an all-out laugh and stroked him.

"I guess I'm right," she said, standing up straight again and removing her hand. She walked over to her purse. "Two thousand, extra fees for anything more than sex. My pussy is golden, I should be charging more. You have my number; use it if you're interested. If not, I'll see you at my next yearly."

She blew a sensual kiss at a dumbfounded Dr. Howard and walked out the door. She kept herself together when she checked out and grabbed her own discharge papers from the receptionist. When she finally reached her Impala she shut the door and gripped the wheel, shaking. There was no doubt in her mind that Dr. Howard would call her, but the reality of it all was shattering.

It will only be for a little bit, she said to herself when Doctor Howard called that same night. *Just until you make enough money to leave.*

But there she was, six months later, getting ready for yet another date. Her clientele had increased. Only rich men with negative STD results were on her roster. The man that night was a brain surgeon who had wanted to take her to a rundown motel that was not too far from her home. He usually took her to penthouse suites or the second home he secretly owned. That night he wanted to live out the fantasy of fucking a poor black damsel in distress. She only agreed because Khiron was out of town, otherwise that would have been too close to home. Although he had eyes on her, it didn't take much money to break his little young soldiers and get them to turn the other cheek. They were rookies.

Once she was fully dressed in a simple, cream-colored mini dress and black pumps, Mocha made her way to the motel room. It only took her twenty minutes to get there, and as soon as she pulled up she received a text on her second cell phone that Khiron knew nothing about.

I'm in room 24.

After she parked her car far enough away from the motel she looked at all the numbers on the doors until she found the room he was in. Knocking softly, she only had to wait a few seconds before she heard footsteps scurrying to the door. The occupant of the room cracked the door open.

"Can I help you?" Charles the brain surgeon said, standing there in jeans and a T-shirt.

"Please!" Mocha faked a tone of panic. "I think somebody is after me. Do you have a phone I can use?"

"Uh, yeah, come right in," Charles welcomed her.

Charles was a short, fat white man who had a fetish for role playing. He was also one of Mocha's lower paying customers. On top of that, she always felt dirty after having his hands all over her body. She decided that after that night she would no longer service his fat, nasty ass.

"Thank you so much!" She stood in front of the bed and waited. When he didn't hand her the phone and instead stared hungrily at her, she furrowed her brow in a pout. "Can I use your phone please?"

"Doesn't it cost to use a pay phone?" Charles grinned and put one of his hands over the bulge in his crotch area.

Mocha gasped and placed her hand over her chest as if appalled by what he was insinuating.

"But sir, I'm not that kind of girl!"

But Charles had already advanced on her, and was slipping his hand up her dress.

"What are you doing out this late with a short dress like this on?"

"I was just out with a friend," Mocha said timidly and backed up until she "accidently" fell on the bed.

Charles grinned at her performance, and his chubby cheeks rose.

"Can I be your friend?" he asked, slipping her shoes off and parting her legs by the knees.

Before she could reply, he put her thong to one side of her vagina and shoved two fingers inside of her.

"Ahh," Mocha grimaced. "Sir, I—"

"Don't be shy, baby," Charles said. "You need to use the phone, don't you?"

Mocha looked into his green eyes and nodded her head. Charles unzipped his pants and let them fall to his ankles. Before anything real happened Mocha looked to her right and saw that her money was sitting neatly on the dresser. He knew the procedure. Mocha looked back to him and saw his tiny penis poking through his boxers.

"Oh, my!" She made her eyes big as saucers. "You're so big."

Charles brushed his blonde hair from his face and mounted her. He raised her dress over her head and threw it to the ground. Not bothering to remove her bra, he popped each nipple out. As he nibbled and slurped away, Mocha tried not to feel sick at the feeling and sight of him on her. Instead she began to moan and pretend that she liked it. While he was defiling her breasts she heard him rip something open. She didn't have to look to know that he was putting on a condom, she smelled it.

"Turn around," he grunted, and of course Mocha obliged.

Charles began to plant wet kisses down her back once her knees were planted on the rough comforter of the bed. When he reached her ass he parted her cheeks and she felt his wet warm tongue start going to town on her asshole.

"Oooohh, yes," Mocha moaned into the pillow.

She couldn't fake the tiny quivers coming from her body. If there was one thing that man could do, it was eat ass. The only sounds heard were her moans and the slurping of his mouth. He was the only man that Mocha had ever met that didn't eat pussy but would lick the shit out of some ass. When he had gotten his fix he inserted his five-inch penis inside of Mochas wetness and began to thrust in and out. Although Mocha barely felt it, she let out a scream like it was the biggest dick she'd ever received in her life. She threw it back at him and he repeatedly slapped her cheeks to see them jiggle.

"You." Slap. "Dirty." Slap. "Black." Slap. "Whore!"

After about ten minutes of the doggie style position he must have gotten tired, because he laid on his back, breathing heavily. Mocha almost threw up at the sight of his sweat drenched T-shirt and face when she straddled him. She began to ride him like a wild woman, cringing inside while he gripped her thighs.

"Such a dirty black bitch," he said again, watching her breasts bounce. His nails dug into her. "Yea. You like that big dick, don't you?

Mocha almost burst out laughing.

"Yes, daddy," she moaned instead.

Charles used his thumb to circle around her clit, and she couldn't deny how good it felt. Soon they were both moaning as she rode him to ecstasy. Mocha felt his dick pulsate and explode inside of her. She then felt herself release, too.

"Ahhh!" they both said in a pleasurable unison.

Breathing heavily, she rolled onto the bed next to him. She knew she wouldn't have to worry about a round two, because minutes later she heard snores coming from beside her. Getting up from the bed, she went to the bathroom to clean and look at herself. After five minutes of being in the bathroom she came back out and put her clothes on. Once she slipped her feet back into her pumps she grabbed her money and was out the door. The drive home was a silent one, and she let her thoughts consume her. The familiar sounds of Detroit kept her focused on the road, and it didn't take long for her to get to where she was going. Pulling into her driveway, she saw that there was somebody sitting on her porch, almost as if they were waiting.

"Who the hell is that?" she asked aloud to herself, unbuckling her seatbelt.

She knew it wasn't Khiron because he had a key. The person stood up when Mocha opened her car door, and she could make out the frame of a woman in designer clothes and heels. Her face was still dark.

"Excuse me, but who the fuck are you?" Mocha put her hand in her purse.

She felt her fingers touch her gun, Lucy, and prepared to aim and shoot. The stranger stepped down from the stoop toward the light by Mocha's garage, and her features became more distinguished. Mocha's heart was beating like a drummer as she tried to catch her breath. The woman before her looked different than she remembered, since she now had a bob haircut, however the sharpness in her deep brown eyes was the same. She was still gorgeous with her five-five frame and Coca-Cola shape. Mocha stared in disbelief and took a deep breath.

"Sadie?"

Chapter 7

For months, I played the scene of when I would finally come face-to-face with Mocha over and over in my head. I wondered what I would do in that moment, how I would feel. There I stood, staring at my former best friend with nothing but hate surging through my veins. I would have given my life for her two times, but when put in the line of fire she proved that she wouldn't do the same for me. My trigger finger twitched, but I told myself to calm down, because unfortunately I needed her. She was soaking in my presence and I saw her eyes linger on my the fresh bob haircut I now rocked. Before I left Miami, after thinking on it for a while, I allowed Devynn to use her scissors on my head. A new look for a new chapter in my life.

"H-how?" she asked, wide-eyed.

"What?" I asked in a low tone, cocking my head. "Do you fuckin' want a hug? What's the matter, Mo? You look like you just saw a ghost!"

"Sadie, I'm so sorry. I never wanted any of that to happen. It wasn't supposed to be like that."

I was unmoved by her words, and the tears in her eyes meant nothing to me. I adjusted the black gloves on my hands and tried to let my anger subside.

"You want to know how I survived, huh?" I chuckled. "You should have paid more attention to Grandma Rae. I have a special heart Mocha, you remember her saying that?"

She nodded her head, and I saw the confusion spread across her face.

"The bullet Khiron put in my chest didn't penetrate it. My heart is on the *opposite* side of my chest, unlike the common person. That's what she meant by saying my heart was special. I found out after the fact of being shot. If Khiron was smart, he would have put more than three bullets in my body," I smirked. "His mistake. But if it hadn't been for Adrianna and Devynn showing up when they did, I would have been dead no question. It took six months of physical therapy and being connected to fuckin' tubes to fully function again."

My finger twitched again, but I clenched my fist. I glared into Mocha's eyes.

"Did it make you happy?" I taunted her calmly. "Watching Ray die?"

Mocha shook her head and let the streams of tears slide down her face. All of the good times that we had together raced through my mind like a video reel. I had entrusted her with everything, and in return she betrayed me.

"We took you in, Mocha!" I yelled into the night. "Bitch, you didn't have one person to live for, and we gave you that! But then you chose a nigga over us?" I took a breath, fighting my tears. "Over *family*? I don't have anybody now, Mocha. Not Grandma Rae, not Ray, nobody! My cousin couldn't even receive a proper burial because there was *nothing* left to bury. For what? For this?"

I began walking toward her and waved my arms in a circular motion.

"Bitch, this nigga got you living out of a fuckin' shoebox, ho'ing on the low," I shook my head. "I could dead your ass, and trust me it's *so* tempting, but I'm not going to."

Mocha looked taken aback, and I smiled. She thought I was there to kill her.

"I can't kill you, actually," I told her. "Just like Khiron used you as his key, *I'm* using you as mine. And I need you to lead me to someone."

"Y-your key to what? And lead you to who?" Mocha asked meekly.

"Kings don't fucking die, remember, Mocha?" I said. "And there's a peasant running my city. I need it back. Marie's missing; I know she's not dead. Tyler isn't going to rest until he finds her."

I was directly in front of her, nose to nose. I nodded my head down the street and she looked toward the bullet proof Hummer that was once Ray's.

"Tyler's alive?" she asked, dumbfounded.

"You're not stupid, Mocha. You know what's up. We had to keep a low profile. But now, it's time to take back what's ours, and you're going to help." I turned my back to her and began to walk away. I stopped and slightly turned my head back. "This meeting? It never happened. The *real* war starts tomorrow. Play your role. You'll be hearing from me soon. Oh, and don't worry. If this doesn't work I *will* kill you, then shoot Khiron's mother's house up and make him come look for me."

I turned my head forward and without another word walked across the street toward where the all black Hummer was parked. The sound of my heels stabbing the concrete kept my emotions in check until I got in the vehicle where Devynn and Adriana sat waiting for me. I motioned for Devynn to pull off as soon as the door was shut.

"What happened?" Adrianna asked, leaning forward from the back seat.

"I'll be contacting her tomorrow," I told them, hoping they wouldn't pry, but of course that was impossible Devynn.

"Yooo," she started. "For a second there I thought you were about to take that bitch out of her misery. I would have left her leaking in front of that raggedy-ass house."

I ignored Devynn and continued looking straight ahead at the familiar scenery. My eyes shifted, falling on the familiar moves of a few young corner boys hitting the block. I couldn't help but shake my head knowing they were moving so close to my grandmother's block. Ray would have never approved. My heart wrenched and I couldn't wait to get out of that part of town, too many happy memories were flooding my brain. Happy memories that I couldn't stand to think about. After seeing Mocha I was past the point of tears. If I succumbed to the emotions washing over me the rage would be too powerful. I'd have to turn around and finish the job early. Instead I focused on the fact that we really needed to keep it pushing. We were hot riding around in Ray's Hummer; anyone native to the area could spot the truck a block away. I didn't want to take any chances of Khiron making any connections.

That night I definitely never planned on making physical contact with Mocha. Tyler's informant in Detroit gave him the information on where she lived and how she was secretly a prostitute at night. The plot twist and irony in that were just too sweet. I couldn't even say I felt sorry for her, at least she wasn't attached to tubes for months out of her life. I was only supposed to be in her house to plant a cell phone and set up surveillance cameras. Breaking into her house was easy; leaving without seeing her was hard. Even though I hated her a piece of me needed to look in her eyes. I needed her to *see* my face when I said what I had to say.

"Go back to the house," I instructed, not wanting to talk about it anymore.

I had a lump in my throat and I needed to get as far away from that neighborhood as possible. The sorrow deep inside my gut was eating away at me. Mocha was my sister, and even though her arrangements were a consequence of her own doing, I couldn't imagine living the way that she was. In a sense we had the same enemy, and he was an ugly son of a bitch, which was why I had to take him down.

Getting into Detroit was probably the trickiest thing we had to do. Legacy hired a theatre makeup artist to transform our appearance, and we created fake identities. We were transformed into three African women coming to Detroit to visit family over the weekend. We were given fake IDs and fake fingerprints to match. The lace front I had to put on was the most uncomfortable thing I had to wear, but the artist really did a great job. I couldn't even recognize myself.

Before I left Miami I made contact with Vinny. I had to. By touching down in Detroit I knew I'd be putting the Italians in the line of fire with the Dominicans by gunning for Khiron. Once informed of my intentions, Vinny arranged for the three of us to get picked up at the airport. When we got inside the limo I smiled once I saw who the driver was.

"You get around, don't you?" I asked.

Victor's response was a wink as he pulled away from the crowded airport. He explained that he was taking us to a home that Ray had secretly built a few months before his murder. It didn't even have an address. After driving for an hour we reached where the house was hidden in the woods. I tried my best to pay attention to direction so that I remembered how to get to and from the house. My eyes watered instantly when I saw it. I had to breathe deeply to keep from choking up at the memory in my head. . . .

"I'm gon' move Grandma Rae out of the hood one day," my sixteen-year-old voice told Ray.

Ray laughed and rubbed his facial hair from where he sat on the bed in my bedroom.

"Grandma Rae isn't going anywhere, shorty. Her soul is in this house, you know that."

We were sitting in my room, watching reruns of The Fresh Prince of Bel-Air before he had to hit the block again. Usually he spent his downtime in the room that he had in the basement of Grandma Rae's house, catching up on his sleep. However, that day he had decided to come and kick it with me for a little bit.

"I'll make her," I said matter-of-factly. "I'm not going to leave her here. I'm going to move her into my dream house. Three stories, finished basement, home movie theatre, a three-car garage, and I want the inside to be classy. None of that tacky stuff that rich people be doing just because they have money."

"Classy, huh?" Ray mocked, raising his eyebrow at me.

"Yes, classy! I'm serious, Ray!" I laughed at his facial expression. "And I want it to be made of brick."

"Yea, 'cause trying to move her from this house is going to be like moving a ton of bricks," Ray chuckled. "All right shorty, I got moves to make, so I'm finna be out. You straight? You need some pocket change?"

As he spoke he pulled out a rolled up stack of hundred-dollar bills and peeled two from it.

"No, I don't need nothing," I said, letting him know I didn't need any money. One of my feet was dangling off my bed and it brushed against a box of merchandise I secretly sold. Everything from designer purses and shoes, I had it to sell. "I keep money."

"I feel you, shorty," Ray gave me a knowing look and kissed me on my forehead. "I love you. I'll see you later."

I remembered watching him walk out of the house with a swag that let the world know how sure of himself he was. I also remember wanting to prove him wrong, I would move Grandma Rae out of the hood. Or so I thought—I never got the chance to. Still, the house before me proved that Ray believed me after all. I stared at my dream home and an overwhelming feeling washed over me.

"Say, you okay?" Devynn asked me, placing a hand on my shoulder.

"I'm okay," I whispered and turned my head so she wouldn't see the tears threatening to fall from my eyes. "I'm okay."

As soon as the vehicle was all the way stopped I was the first one out of it. Before I could walk up to the door Victor reached his hand out of his window so that he could hand me the keys. Clenching them in my hand, I walked slowly to the front door and tried to look inside. The stained glassed windows made that impossible. Not able to contain my curiosity I unlocked the door and walked through it. I didn't take two steps before I felt Adrianna's hand on my shoulder, holding me back. Both she and Devynn had their guns drawn when they stepped around me to scope the house out. Once they were done making their rounds they came back to where I stood in the foyer, telling me nothing seemed out of place. After that I relaxed a bit and went on search for something I knew Ray had built within the house, the artillery room. I knew my cousin like the back of my hand, because it didn't take me long to find it. I knew he wouldn't make it easy for just anyone, it was in a hidden room behind a wall in the basement. Looking at all the weapons in that room, an outsider might have mistaken Ray for a terrorist. From automatic guns to grenades, Ray had it all. He wasn't going to put me in a house with only the burner on my hip.

In the garages, there were already three cars. There were two Mercedes CL600 coupes; one black and one white. For Mocha and me I was sure. There was also an all black Hummer; Ray's Hummer. It was shiny like it had been cleaned, and I felt like a part of me was born again. I knew Khiron had probably torched Ray's Escalade, but the Hummer was his second baby. It was all mine now.

Devynn, Adrianna, and I devised a plan on what was going on with the new kingpin of Detroit, and any information on his business dealings with the Dominicans. It was Adrianna's idea to bug Mocha's house, but it was my mission to complete. And I had completed it without getting her blood on my hands. Now all that was left to do was to be patient and wait.

Chapter 8

It had been a week since Mocha had seen or heard from Sadie, but it didn't matter. Just the knowledge of her survival gave her a strange feeling of peace. It gave her more hope than the stash of money building under the boards in her tiny bedroom. Mocha lay silently in her queen-sized bed watching the sun shine through her open blinds. She didn't have to look outside to know that Khiron's guard dogs were watching her house. During the day she never had any motivation to get out of the house and do anything because she knew Khiron's goons would be close behind her. She felt like a child on a short leash. Khiron made it his business to try and keep a close eye on Mocha and at the same time, he tried to keep her out of the loop.

Mocha pretended to not know anything that was going on around her; however Khiron must have forgotten who she was. She noticed everything, especially when it came to him. He was so unpredictable that she wanted to see any curveball coming from a mile away. He was truly a Dr. Jekyll, Mr. Hyde kind of man. She couldn't count how many times she had planned to murder him when he came to her home, but she was too much of a coward behind him. He made her feel weak the moment he was in her presence. He had her mind gone, and although she did have a gun, she knew one wrong move would mean the worst for her.

At first after he killed Ray a major drought overcame the city because nobody was getting any money. The product going around the city was horrible, and many customers complained that the high didn't last. Even the most loyal customers turned to getting high off of other drugs because of the low grade of cocaine Khiron had at first. That was something that changed quickly, though. Mocha didn't know the specifics, she just knew that somehow the Dominican cartel had stepped in and offered Khiron a permanent place in their business. Mocha remembered hearing him on the phone talking to his right hand man, Tyreek, and telling him that Don Rivera promised to supply him with whatever he needed as long as Detroit was his main venue of business.

As time progressed, she started to see his operation grow into something much bigger than even he thought it would be. Slowly but surely, the movement in Detroit was reborn, except it was different. Khiron had gone back to the old ways of the kingpins before him. He set up trap houses around the city and had his boys on the corners of every block. It was known that Khiron was the one who had murdered Ray, so it wasn't hard for him to get the people to go along with his movement. It was the rule of trade, everyone knew that when the current kingpin died, the throne was up for grabs. But he didn't make that possible for anyone else. Soon, there wasn't a major drug capital that didn't know Khiron's name. He was known as the man who had brought down the kings, and for that, the streets didn't know whether to respect or to fear him.

Mocha noticed the change in his evil demeanor, and it was apparent that he was relishing in Detroit. Her city. The more money he got, the more sadistic he became. The man she fell in love with was dead and gone, only to be replaced by the devil himself. The only time Mocha saw him was when he needed arm candy to compliment his outer appearance or when he wanted some pussy from her. Whichever it was, her nights always ended the same, alone once more in her room. He always told her that if she tried to run away he would find her. And when he did, the fate he would subject her to would be worse than death.

In the distance the faint sound of her door opening caught Mocha off guard. Alarmed, she sat up in her purple bedding because she knew that Khiron was the only other person who had a key. Straining her ears toward the sound, she hoped that she was just imagining things. She wasn't. The sound of footsteps were clear as day, and they were heading straight toward her bedroom. She hurried to lay back down and tried to force her body to go limp. She clenched her eyes shut and listened to the footsteps until they found their destination. Her room door creaked open and she tried to even her breathing. When she felt the person's presence get closer to her bed, she pretended to give the illusion of a deep sleep.

"You don't have to fake sleep, shawty," a deep voice that didn't belong to Khiron said. "It's just me."

Mocha's eyes shot open when she recognized the familiar Georgia accent and sighed her relief.

"'Reek! I thought you were still in Atlanta!" Mocha stood up from the bed to face Khiron's right hand man.

"That nigga called me back, we have some business to handle," he smiled kindly down at her, flashing his pearly whites.

Despite the cruelty Khiron showed her, Tyreek still went out of his way to be good to her. He still treated her the way he did when things between she and Khiron were good. When Khiron left bruises on her body, he was the one bringing the medical attention in to nurse her back to health. Through all of the cruelties from Khiron, Tyreek was the only source of kindness that she received.

No matter what the circumstances were, he never looked at her any differently, or so it seemed, anyway. She didn't know if he was being genuine or if he was just trying to keep an eye on her for Khiron. Maybe he just flat out felt sorry for her, but either way she was grateful. Mocha caught him staring at her a couple of times, but the look in his eyes was always one that she could not read. They didn't hold the normal thirst of the usual man that eyed her, but seemed more intrigued.

Mocha looked down and saw he was holding a few shopping bags. She stared at the tall, chocolate man before her and a smile crept to her face. He rocked a brush cut and had a strong jaw bone structure. His eyes were a deep, chocolate brown and his lips were pink and full. She wondered what they would feel like pressed against hers. He was dressed casually in a pair of Robin jeans and a silky white V-neck. She wanted to ask him why he was so good to her when his right hand man treated her like scum, but it wouldn't have been her first time asking it. He always gave her the same answer.

"You're not a bad person, shawty," he would say.

Instead, she tore her eyes away from his handsome face and nodded toward the bags.

"For me?" she asked, and he set them on the bed for her.

She ripped into them and found three gorgeous designer dresses with three matching pairs of heels. Once she saw the items she rolled her eyes and sighed heavily. She already knew what they meant. She placed her hand on her hip and cocked her head in annoyance.

"When does he need me, Tyreek?"

"In two days," Tyreek said, looking into Mocha's flawless face and admiring her beauty.

If circumstances were different, he knew that Mocha would have been wife. Not his wifey, but the woman with the ring. He had been in love once, and the lifestyle he lived was what had gotten her killed. Tyreek knew he would never have to worry about that with Mocha, she handled her own. He knew about her, that is why she had earned mad respect with him. She was everything that he wanted in a woman. Mocha was thorough and they would have been great together. Unfortunately, that was a line that neither one of them could or would cross. Since he rocked with Khiron, Mocha was the enemy, which meant he was supposed to hate her, too. But he couldn't. He would never be able to respect her decision to sell her loyalty for love, but he understood why she did it. The thought of a life including never-ending money, without having to lift a finger, was enticing. That's the dream that Khiron sold her, and she had used her last dollar to buy it. The way Khiron had her living was the worst torture to someone of Mocha's caliber. He might as well have just killed her.

"Who is he meeting with?" Mocha asked, holding one of the dresses in the air from where she sat on her bed.

"Don Rivera," Tyreek said.

The dress instantly dropped from her hands at the mention of the head of the Dominican cartel.

"What?" Mocha asked, wide-eyed.

Mocha knew that the Dominicans gave Khiron mad work, but she also knew that Don Rivera rarely left his comfortable home in Azua. Khiron usually did business through Robert, Don's trusted informant. Once Robert came to Detroit he proved just how far Don's reach was. Within a day the Dominicans had the city on lock, and Khiron's business ventures began to flourish. The Last Kings was something of the past, and Ray's name was one spoken with caution in his own city.

"Yes," Tyreek confirmed. "The Dominicans are looking to expand their work. The Italians are still flourishing greatly, even without The Last Kings operation. In a war, that's not good. It must be something big, though, 'cause dude never leaves his house."

"Two days?" Mocha shook her head. "Where?"

"You know I can't tell you that, Mocha," Tyreek said reminding Mocha of his allegiance to Khiron. "Just be ready at seven o'clock on Friday night. A driver will be by to pick you up."

Mocha stared into his face blankly, trying not to give off any emotion. She knew something he didn't know. Ever since Mocha saw Sadie it felt like she was walking on eggshells, wondering when she would strike. She felt hope, but she also felt fear, simply because she knew that Sadie would show no mercy. It felt like the days were being numbered, but she knew she deserved to die. However, Tyreek, who had been so good to her, didn't deserve death. He was just loyal to the wrong side.

"Okay," was all she said, and Tyreek gave her a strange look.

"You good?" He asked.

He knew she would say yes even if the answer was no. Khiron was a twisted man. Instead of killing Mocha he was tempting her to kill herself. Everyday he wanted her to wish herself to death, and that was a torture fit for no one.

"Yea," Mocha answered, wondering why he was still there. "Was there something else you wanted?"

She stood up from her bed so that she could take the dresses and the shoes to her closet. Tyreek silently watched her. The cotton shorts she wore accented her thick hips, and for just a second he let his mind wander. He wondered how it would feel to pin her down and drill into her. He wanted to know what her voice would sound like calling his name. He smirked at her and shook his head.

"Nah," he said. "I'm out. You have my number if you need me. I'm in town until Sunday."

"Khiron is here too?" Mocha asked, even though she knew if he was in town Tyreek wouldn't be at her house.

"Nah," he said again. "He'll be here tomorrow, though."

Fuck, Mocha thought as she waved good-bye.

When Mocha heard the door shut she sighed to herself. She went to peek out of the window and saw Tyreek's car driving off. She almost smiled, but then she saw the all-black Mercedes Benz parked in its usual spot across the street from her house. Clenching her teeth, she forced herself to take a deep breath as she glared at the car. She thought about the favors she had to trade to get them to let her free for a few hours in the night and wanted to throw up. The things they made her do for her freedom proved to her that she was never free. She could run, but she knew Khiron would find her. The only vehicle she had was registered to him and nobody came to Mocha's house if he didn't know them. She knew the only way Sadie knew to come to the house when nobody was standing guard was if Sadie had been watching her for a while. Either way it went, her life wasn't hers. Stepping away from the window she walked over to her dresser with a purpose. Kneeling down, she reached under it and felt around until her hand located what it was looking for. Wrapping her fingers around the butt of the gun she yanked her hand back, breaking the object back from the tape that held it in place. It was a gun that she had purchased in secret. It didn't mean as much as the pistol Ray gave her that she'd left at Grandma Rae's old house, but it made her feel safe. She stared at it in her hand and thought about what she was about to do. It was time to just end it all. All of the hurt, but most of all, the suffering. She slowly brought the loaded weapon up to her temple with her right hand and placed her finger on the trigger. Mocha knew that with one jerk of her finger it would all be over.

She had never really thought about death because she was too busy living. There was still so much that she wanted to do with and in her life. Yes, it was true that Mocha loved Sadie like a sister, but at the end of the day Sadie wasn't her sister. No matter how welcome Sadie and Ray tried to make her feel, it didn't change the fact that she always felt alone. Mocha didn't talk about her feelings much, so of course Sadie didn't know how Mocha really felt. She never wanted to be a part of a drug cartel, but she went with it because of the money that was involved. The plan was to get in the game for a little while. Just until she had enough saved up to do what she wanted to and live comfortably as well. Everything changed when she met Khiron. She fell in love, and in a twisted way she still loved him. It hurt her that he couldn't see past his past to see that her feelings for him had been genuine. Yet she knew that this was just how the game went, and there was nothing that she could do to change it.

By that point, warm, salty tears were streaming down Mocha's face. She was thinking about the things Khiron would do to her after the meeting, and her grip on Lucy tightened. It was time to finally give in to what Khiron wanted: her lying in a pool of her own blood. She had always done what people wanted her to do, for once she wished she would have chosen for herself.

"*So choose yourself,*" she said to herself. "*Run. You have to get away from here.*"

Her arm trembled as it slowly lowered until the gun was hanging loosely at her side. It was time for her to be selfish. As messed up as things were, she had already chosen her side. Although it had ended poorly, she chose Khiron over Sadie. She knew Sadie would never forgive her. They wouldn't be best friends again; things would never go back to how they used to be. They were enemies.

As soon as she was of no use, Mocha already knew that she would be disposed of, so why wait around for that to happen?

Thinking deeply, Mocha sat down on her bed and at that moment made a decision. She would help Sadie do whatever she needed to do, and hoped that it would stir up enough commotion in Detroit to avert Khiron's attention. That was when she would run. That was when she would be free again.

Chapter 9

"Bitch, if you don't hurry up and bag that shit up!" A young man barked down at a woman dressed in nothing but a bra and a pair of boy short panties.

Using his left palm, he threw her head down so harshly it almost hit the brown table that she was kneeling in front of. The woman sat back up straight and nodded her head without looking up at the man who had just put his hands on her. She wanted to roll her eyes and tell him to get the fuck on somewhere, but she knew things would escalate quickly after that. Instead she kept her mouth shut under the mask she wore on her face.

She and three other girls sat on the living room floor of a two-bedroom apartment bagging up sacks of cocaine. Khiron expected a certain dollar amount produced from all of the work in locations he had hidden around Atlanta. That night the shipment had been bigger than expected and it was taking a little longer to complete the task. It also didn't help that she had done a line before she started bagging.

"Marie just high, that's all," Lisha, one of the other women around the table snitched. "I don't even know why y'all got her in here with us. We tryna get money, and she's turnin' into a cokehead."

"Bitch, you got me fucked up," Marie said back, surprised at Lisha's outburst. She set the contents in her hands down so that she could slap the chocolate-skinned woman in front of her. "You're just a hating-ass ho like these other two bitches."

Marie waved her finger at the two women, named Rissa and Bunny. Both of them instantly took offense to her words and looked at Marie like she was off her rocker.

"Who this yellow slut think she talking to?" Rissa asked, throwing the bag in her hand down.

Before any of them could get at each other Marie felt a hand snatch her up by the arm and yank her to her feet.

"All you bitches shut the fuck up before I air this bitch out!" the man gripping her arm shouted. "Me and my niggas don't want to hear all that."

At the sight of the Mac 11 in his hand all sound ceased to exist in the room. Hearing the commotion from the next room, two men came from the bedroom they were in. Each had a game controller in one hand and a pistol in the next.

"Everything good in here, Vince?" one of the masked men asked.

"Hell, nah, shit ain't good," Vince said, snatching Marie closer to him. "I think this ho in here getting high off the product."

The drugs coursing through her system made it hard for Marie to stand without swaying slightly. Her eyes tried to focus on Vince's face, but he was so close to her it kept going in and out of focus.

"Man, this ho is high as fuck," Vince smacked his lips, looking at her dilated pupils. He snatched the mask from her face and squeezed her cheeks, forcing her mouth open. He took one look at her tongue and knew that Lisha was telling the truth. Putting his cold gun to her temple, he sneered in her face. "Give me one good reason why I shouldn't kill you right now."

Marie knew that Lisha had set her up by snitching, after all she was the one who snuck Marie the drugs in the first place. Since the day she had been brought to stay in the house Khiron kept them all in, it was apparent that no one there liked her. Growing up in the hood before

Tyler moved her into her own spot, Marie used to hear stories about Bitch Houses. They were houses where kingpins kept their whores. These were women that bagged up the work, smuggled it in and out of state, and took the wrap for any and everything. She would have never really believed that they existed had she not been living in one for the past year. Marie had so much sorrow brewing inside of her heart it didn't take long for her to start playing with her nose. It made everything around her easier to cope with. Soon after being brought to live in a house with nine other women, she learned that the best way to stay alive was to do whatever she was told. If they told her to jump, she jumped. If they told her to cross the border with bags of cocaine stuffed in her pussy and ass, she did it. If they told her to lay down and open her legs . . . she did it. She looked into Vince's eyes and already knew what he wanted. Slowly, she took off her bra and exposed her light breasts to the room.

Vince's eyes traveled to the pink nipples he'd tasted many times before. Even if Lisha hadn't opened her mouth, he was going to take Marie into the back room and wear her out. Whenever a set of girls were dropped off to his location to clear it out he hoped that Marie was one of them. Out of all the whores he had sexed in the house, she was his favorite. The moment he saw her walk into the apartment that night he knew she was high. The women didn't have to take off their clothes to bag, but when Vince was in charge he made them. The first time Vince had laid eyes on Marie she was petite with few curves, but now she was thick in all the right places. He didn't need to know that it was because of the birth control Khiron forced them all to be on; all he cared about were her plump ass cheeks poking out on the sides. He had always loved him a redbone, and her full pink lips made him wish his dick had access to them all the time.

Her eyes were so low, and without trying, every look she gave him turned him on. He nudged her head with his gun and nodded his head to the room that wasn't being used at the moment.

"Go," he instructed, and then turned to the other men in the room. "Make sure these hoes finish out here."

He followed behind Marie into the room and flicked the light off. Once the door was shut he proceeded to grope her all over her body. She couldn't make out a thing in the room, so she just stood still and let him squeeze and lick all over her.

"Take these panties off," he said, tugging at the cotton covering her best assets.

She did as she was told and bent down so that she could slide her panties off. The moment she stood back up, Vince cupped her pussy with his right hand, using his middle finger to part her lips. Marie was so high and his touch sent tingles down her spine. It felt so good to her and the jewel between her legs did what it was supposed to do. Feeling how wet she was growing, Vince used his middle finger to circle her clit while he bent down and popped her nipple in his mouth. Marie threw her head back and allowed his fingers to dive in and out of her. When he made the "come here" motion with his fingers to rub against her G-Spot she felt her clit swell. The feeling of his tongue circling her areola and his fingers working their magic relentlessly was too much for her to handle.

"Ahhhh!" she moaned when she couldn't hold her orgasm in any longer. She squirted her juices all over his hand and dropped to her knees, trembling.

Vince didn't let her catch her breath before he was shoving his eight inches of thickness in her mouth. Gripping the back of her head, he guided her as she slurped and slobbered all over his shaft. He fucked her throat and jaws rough purposely because he wanted to hear her choke on his tip. She took it like a champ for a good ten minutes before he made her stop and forced her to her feet by her hair. He grabbed her arm, spun her around and threw her forward. Before Marie could brace herself for the hard floor, she was surprised when she landed on a soft bed. Marie heard the condom wrapper ripping behind her and Vince fumbling to put it on. She was supposed to be on a beach somewhere right now, not on the bed having sex with a drug dealer. Right before he entered her from behind she closed her eyes shut and thought back to the day her life changed forever.

"W-where's Tyler?"

Those were the first words out of Marie's mouth when she finally came to. She was laying on a bed in a hotel room. The clothes on her body as well as the hair on her head were damp, and when she tried to move her arms she found that she couldn't. She started to panic when she saw that her wrists and ankles had rope around them, bounding her to the bed. Slowly but surely, her memories were coming back to her, jumbled and mixed up. The last thing she remembered was getting into a car accident with her brother. Her eyes tried to focus on the room around her and she tried to figure out where she was. Head throbbing like she'd been hit with a ton of bricks, her eyes frantically scanned the room and she tried to will the ringing in her ears away. She made out the bodies of five men, all wearing black suits and all wearing the same emotionless look on their face. Marie was too terrified to move and the menacing atmosphere of the room caused her bottom lip to tremble when she repeated her question.

"Where is Tyler?" That time she tried to steady her voice, but her fear snuck its way there anyway.

"He's dead," a bored tone said bluntly.

Marie's eyes shot to the foot of the bed where a man towered staring directly into her eyes. There was something about the coldness of his eyes and hard expression that made Marie's heart freeze over. He was easy on the eyes and wore his hair in a tapered fade. He rubbed his chin and gave a small laugh.

"I killed him," he took a step to the side of the bed and sat down on it. "And I'm going to kill you, too, if you don't tell me what I need to know."

Marie didn't grasp his last sentence right away because his first was still replaying in her head. All at once, the images of the crash were coming back to her. She remembered trying to get to her brother so that she could protect him somehow, but there was no point. She now knew why she couldn't get the ringing out of her head. She swallowed hard once the guilt settled in. Tyler was dead because he was trying to get her to safety. She tried to bite back her tears that came with the heaviness of her heart.

"W-who are you?" Marie forced herself to say. "And why did you want my brother dead?"

"My name is Khiron, shawty," he answered simply, in a low tone. "And your brother is dead because any friend of my enemy is my enemy."

His voice was smooth, and he never took his eyes off of hers. He smiled at her and used his fingers to trace her exposed calf, causing her to flinch. He smiled.

"Now that you have asked all of your allotted questions, I have some of my own."

"I don't know anything that you need to know, I swear," Marie started to sob and take brisk breaths. "Please don't kill me."

Khiron looked down at Marie's pleading face and turned his nose up slightly. Without saying another word, he stood to his feet and looked to the five men, silently gaving them all their instructions. He pulled the desk chair up to the foot of the bed and one of his men placed a black briefcase on the bed.

"Please don't kill me. Pleeeease. Please," Marie begged through her sobs. Her face was completely drenched from her tears and she prayed that God would show mercy on her soul. When she saw what the man pulled from the briefcase she let out a blood curdling scream and tried to fight against her restraints. "Noooo! Noooo!"

The man stuffed the ball of the gag that he'd removed from the brief case in Marie's mouth while another one held her face still so that it could be secured. Soon all that could be heard from her mouth were muffled shouts. Khiron watched as his men tortured Marie for hours until the bed under her was stained in blood. He asked her questions about The Last Kings operation in hopes to get another one up on them, however there was no use. The pain that he inflicted on her no man would be able to withstand without giving him some sort of information. When the only thing she could tell him was her name, no matter how badly it hurt, he finally called his men off. He started to believe that she was truly just the kid sister of a hustler. Too bad he still didn't have much sympathy for her—in his eyes she was still his enemy.

"Everybody but Brandon, leave," Khiron told his men. "Make sure nobody is poking their noses around here, and if they are, you know what to do."

"Yea, boss?" Brandon, a caramel stocky man with a brush cut.

"She doesn't know anything," Khiron said, staring at the barely conscious woman on the bed.

Marie's eyes were almost swollen shut, and if she thought her body was sore before, the pain she felt now was excruciating. She was positive her jaw was broken, and she kept choking on her own blood.

"You want me to finish this bitch off?"

Khiron pondered over Brandon's question for a moment. He was angry that he had wasted his time questioning Marie, and usually that was cause for a bullet in the head. Still, he didn't think he would be satisfied. He wanted everyone to suffer continuously, like he had for years, and he had the perfect place that had use for a woman like her.

"Nah," Khiron said, watching Marie slowly fall into unconsciousness. "Clean her up and take her to the house back to Atlanta."

"Anything you say, boss man." Brandon nodded his head already knowing what "house" Khiron was referring to.

"One more thing," Khiron said before he left the room. "As soon as she's healthy, dope her up."

Marie snapped out of her high flashback just as Vince was grunting like a wild animal behind her. She knew that was a for sure sign that he had gotten his nut off, and she was relieved. She waited until she heard him zipping his pants and fastening his belt before she stood up from the bed.

"Damn that pussy good, girl," Vince said and touched her wetness one more time. "Now get the fuck up and get back out there. Don't wash up, niether, keep that pussy wet. One of my niggas might wanna fuck before y'all leave."

Once again, Marie did as she was told. She put her panties back on and walked shamelessly back out of the room. She scooped her bra up off the floor where she had dropped it and knelt back down at the table once it was securely in place. She ignored the girls and went back to bagging, and Vince went back to counting money on the dining room table like nothing had just happened. A year ago, Marie was a girl with her own mind. Now she was somebody's property.

Chapter 10

Before Khiron left Atlanta he always stopped at his main trap house and the house that he kept his whores in. The girls were locked in their rooms as usual, and the only one with freedom to roam the house was his oldest girl, Lisha. When he was assured that everything was good he walked out of the double doors of the large house to a tan Chevy Tahoe waiting for him in the driveway. Khiron handed his suitcase to the driver that stood holding the door to the backseat open and hopped it. When it pulled away from the house, it stopped next to a gold Lexus ES 350 parked curbside directly in front of the house.

"You can take them out somewhere to eat later," Khiron said when he rolled down his window. "My counts came back lovely. Treat these bitches to some steak or something. Hoes love steak."

The two goons sitting inside the vehicle chuckled but nodded their heads before Khiron pulled off into the day. Little did he know that while he was flying to Detroit to handle some business, somebody had snuck into Atlanta to finish theirs. Tyler sat in his rental car a good distance away, watching Khiron through the dark Ray Bans on his face. He couldn't make out what they were saying to each other, but he saw Khiron's arm extend from the back of the truck and throw a set of keys into the passenger side of the Mercedes before he drove away. Tyler and his own goons leaned back in their seats when the truck passed them so they weren't seen. When it was out of sight from the neighborhood, they sat back up and got ready.

Tyler screwed the silencer on his pistol with black gloves on his hands and checked his clip. He looked over to the passenger seat at a man that had been his and Ray's friend since childhood. His loyalty had never wavered, not even with the fall of The Last Kings. Looney was thorough and it was him who had Tyler removed from the hospital. Looney had also been the one to orchestrate Tyler's fake death to the public. Besides Ray, Looney was the only other person that Tyler trusted. He wasn't a part of The Last Kings, but he was affiliated just off GP. When his daughter and her mother were murdered, Looney got out of the game, but he was still an important asset to have around. Not only was his aim as nice as his heart was black, he was knowledgeable about everything and place.

Once Looney was notified by Ray that Tyler was in the hospital, he showed up shortly after Ray left. He didn't want the news that his boy was still alive to hit the streets, so he removed him from the hospital. He paid a nice chunk of change to have any record of his admittance erased from every system, and any video recording of him entering to be burned. Once Tyler got his strength back, Looney he saw how distraught his man was over his baby sister. Not wanting Tyler to feel a loss that deep again he agreed to get back in the game one last time.

"You ready my nigga?" Looney asked in a gruff voice, rubbing his short beard.

In response, Tyler pulled the black mask on his head over his face. Looney followed suit. Tyler looked to the two young goons he'd brought along with him in the back seat.

"Y'all know what to do," Tyler said.

Tyler and Looney were out the car within five seconds. They were bold and fearless. When it came to war you ran up on anybody, broad daylight or not, and Tyler was a loose cannon operating on nothing but revenge. As they advanced on the Lexus they heard the rental car start up and pull off. The red Dodge Avenger slowed down when it got to the Mercedes, getting the driver and the passenger's attention. That distraction was all Tyler and Looney needed as they took their final steps toward the vehicle. Tyler's men then pulled off, and by the time Khiron's watch dogs realized, the car was a decoy it was too late.

"Shit!" the fat driver exclaimed when he saw the masked men.

He tried to reach for the gun on his lap, but Tyler put two neat bullets in his skull, rocking him to sleep forever. Blood splattered the interior of the car as the bullets made their exit out the back of his head. Looney had already slumped the passenger and was reaching inside to grab the keys that were lying in his lap. Tyler knew that the other two were doubling back around the corner to clean up the mess so he didn't wait to jet toward the front door. Looney threw Tyler the keys, and it only took Tyler one try to unlock it. He motioned for Looney to go first with his hands and Looney entered the house, ducked down with his gun drawn. Tyler looked back, making sure nobody was watching the scene, and then followed after Looney. They moved so swiftly that you could barely make out their footsteps, but they paused when they were about to pass the doorway to what Tyler supposed was the kitchen. They heard the tunes of a song being hummed, but Tyler knew it wasn't Marie humming it. Tyler peeked around the corner and saw a short, plump woman in a maid uniform dancing to whatever music was coming from her ear buds. Quietly, they made their way past and continued their search throughout the big house. Every door Tyler passed he would notice it's double bolted lock, and it enraged him.

This nigga got my baby sis living like a prisoner, Tyler thought.

Even if she wanted to run she wouldn't have even had a chance. She would never be able to get out the house.

"Oh my God!" They heard a shriek to the left.

A thick woman with a pretty face bounded down a staircase in only a T-shirt and ran straight into the masked intruders. Her eyes were wide open and she tried to scream in hopes to get somebody's attention. Turning back around she tried to run back up the stairs, but Looney was too quick for her. He snatched her up by the weave ponytail hanging from the top of her head and yanked her back down the stairs. She opened her mouth to scream again, but Looney jammed his gun inside of it.

"Ah, ah, ah," he told her shaking his head. "That wouldn't be a very smart thing to do when somebody has a gun, now would it?"

Fearing for her life, the woman shook her head quickly with the gun in her mouth. She knew these men couldn't be anyone who worked for Khiron. She could tell by his accent that he wasn't even from Atlanta.

"Now, I'ma remove this," Looney wiggled the gun slightly. "But if you scream again I'm going to pull the trigger. Understand?"

The woman nodded her head slowly and stared at Looney with untrusting eyes. When he did what he said he would he placed a finger to her lips.

"Whose house is this?"

"This is the whore house," she said. "We don't know nothin'. Khiron don't keep shit here if you after his money."

"Whore house?" Tyler swole up on the woman and put his hand around her neck.

"Y-yes," the woman choked, pulling at Tyler's strong hand with both of hers. "We just hoes. We just do whatever they tell us to do and run these drugs. Please! I-I can't breathe!"

Tyler didn't care about her lack of oxygen, he was too enraged that Khiron not only had Marie working for him, but he had subjected her to a life that most women never come back from. Mentally and physically. He pressed his gun to the woman's temple and cocked it.

"Tell me where all the rooms are and the names of the women in them," Tyler barked. "Now!"

"Rissa," the woman gasped for air. "R-Rissa is upstairs with me. Candy is d-down the hall. Elisa is u-upstairs too by the bathroom. Marie is in the basement."

As soon as she said Marie's name he let her neck go and Looney hit her in the temple with the butt of his weapon. She crumbled to the floor, passed out, and the men hastily hurried past her.

"I think I saw some stairs this way," Looney said, leading Tyler through the back of the house.

Sure enough, they came across a stairway that led to the basement of the home. At the bottom of the staircase was a big black door. With his gun drawn, Tyler flew down the stairs, two at a time, with Looney right behind him. Tyler used the same key that he used to open the front door to open that one. He caught his breath when the door opened and he saw the room. It was clearly decorated for a woman. The walls were beige and the furniture was dark brown. There weren't any pictures on the walls, but there was a fifty inch flat screen TV hanging and underneath it was a glass cabinet full of DVDs. A long wooden dresser was posted along the wall to his right with a tall mirror. On top of the dresser lay an array of makeup, designer perfumes, and jewelry. Confused, Tyler turned his head and saw the walk in closet on his left. He saw designer shopping bags and clothes hanging; some still with the price tags.

"Aye man," Looney whispered grabbing Tyler's shoulder.

Looney pointed his finger toward the bed, and when Tyler's eyes fell on the silhouette figure laying on it, it felt like his heart had stopped. Next to the bed his eyes brushed over a plate that still had white powder on it. He watched the figure breathe and many emotions washed over him. A part of him had felt that he would never see his sister again, but there she was. Looney had once again come through for Tyler. If it wasn't for his keen ears in the streets, Tyler would have never known about the house that Khiron kept women in. It wasn't known for sure that Marie would be there, but it was his last hope. That year had been full of so many disappointments, and he had to at least try. Whenever he thought he had her, he didn't. Getting his hopes up that time was something he told himself he just wouldn't do. But standing there, watching his baby sister exhale her breath, sent new life into him.

"Marie," he spoke in a deep voice that startled her out of her sleep.

She jumped up and prepared to scream when she saw the two masked men in her room holding guns. Her low eyes gave away the fact that she was coming out of her high, and she swayed so badly on her bed that she had to put her palm down to steady herself.

"Chill, sis," Tyler said, trying to calm her down from under his mask. "Has it been that long since you heard my voice?"

He walked toward the bed, sat beside her, and removed his mask revealing his identity. Marie stared at him for a moment and blinked, because surely her eyes were playing tricks on her. She reached and touched the man's face before her and saw that he was real.

"Tyler?" she whispered, and her lips quivered. "Is that really you?"

Before she knew it, she had jumped into her brother's arms. She clung tightly to her brother and sobbed uncontrollably into his neck. Tyler hugged her tightly too, as if he feared that if he let her go she would disappear into thin air.

"I thought they killed you," Marie leaned back and looked tearfully into her brother's face.

She saw a scar the on top of his head that wasn't there before, and she knew it was from the bullet that she thought had taken his life. Other than that, and the tired look in his eyes, he didn't look different at all.

"You know it would've taken more than some bullets to put this nigga under," Looney's gruff voice said as he removed his mask.

"Loon!" Marie exclaimed and went to hug him.

Looney noticed that her balance was a little off when he let her go, so he tried to hold her steady. He shot a look at Tyler and Tyler clenched his teeth. Tyler knew what went on in whore houses, and he knew that the boss used drugs as a tool to make the girls obedient. Marie had been gone for over a year, and if she had been in that house for that whole time frame it was inevitable that she was a junkie. But Tyler didn't care about that. He would get her clean as soon as he got her out of there, but the first step was leaving with her and never losing sight of her again.

Marie hurried to shut the door, not wanting any of the housekeepers to see the door open and to notify Khiron. She felt something that she thought had died within her heart: hope. The tears streamed freely down her face as she looked at her brother, alive and well. She never thought she'd see his face again.

"Grab your shit, Marie, it's time to go home," Tyler said to her.

She nodded her head and quickly went to her closet to throw some clothes on. Her freedom was so close she could taste it at the tip of her tongue. It had been a day that she dreamt of every night. She stopped packing when she got to the nightstand where the plate with her cocaine was. She looked at it longingly before seeing that Tyler and Looney were watching her.

"I'm–I'm," she tried to get out the words, but she was too embarrassed. "I don't know who I am anymore."

Tyler wrapped his arms around her and nestled her now long hair.

"This isn't you, Marie," he told her. "I'm back. I'm going to get you all the help that you need. I promise. Ain't nobody going to hurt you ever again, you hear me?"

His phone started to vibrate when she nodded into his shirt. He almost sent the call straight to voice mail, but he saw who it was so he answered it.

"You got her?" Sadie's smooth voice came through the receiver after Tyler said hello.

"Yeah," Tyler responded. "We'll be back soon."

"Good," Sadie said. "Because we need you. Khiron is meeting with Don Rivera in two days."

Tyler was thrown off for a second. He knew exactly who Don Rivera was, but he also knew that he was a man who didn't leave his home often. The fact that he was coming to the states signified that the beef between the Dominicans and the Italians was real.

"Damn," Tyler said.

"I know. I can't say much over the phone, but I need you here ASAP. See you soon."

Sadie hung up the phone before Tyler could respond. He let Marie go and stared at the phone in his hand for a second.

"What's going on, Ty?" Marie asked, seeing the change in her brother's face. "Why do you look like that?"

Tyler briefly filled her in on everything that had happened in the past year. She already knew of Ray's death and Mocha's betrayal. She felt great relief in knowing that Sadie was still alive as well. However, hearing about the feud between the Italians and the Dominicans made her take a step back within herself. She now knew why Khiron had left, and she understood what Sadie was trying to do. When Tyler was done speaking, she closed her eyes briefly and then opened them again. When she opened them there were once again tears there. But that time, she wasn't crying tears of joy.

"I can't go, Ty," she said firmly.

"What?" Tyler looked at her like she was crazy. "Finish getting your shit, Marie. We have to go. We've already been here too long."

"I can't go with you," Marie repeated. "Not now."

She watched her brother's face change from confusion to understanding.

"I'm not happy here," Marie started, "but I'm safe. If you take me now, then somebody will notify Khiron of my absence and tell him I'm missing. He'll know. Out of all the girls here, I'm the only one that goes missing? He knows my brother was connected to The Last Kings, and everybody who even cares about my existence is supposed to be dead. If I come up missing you will lose the element of surprise. Everything Sadie has worked for would get fucked up. So I can't go."

"No," Tyler said, but his voice was feeble. He knew she was right. "I came here to find you and—"

"And you found me!" Marie interrupted. "I'm safe here. You've always protected me from the game, so now it's my turn to protect you *in* it."

"She's right, bro," Looney reluctantly chimed in. "It's a fucked up reality, but she's right. If we take her, that's gon' be a big ass red flag to them niggas."

Tyler's mind was reeling at the reality of the situation and the fact that they were right. His mind was telling him to leave and go back to Detroit, but his heart kept him planted right there in Atlanta.

"I'm not going anywhere, Ty," Marie walked up to him and put her hand on his solemn face. "I've been here since the day you started looking for me, you just didn't know. Now you know where to come back to. Go. Come back for me."

Marie choked up on her last word and Tyler used his knuckle to stroke her cheek. Although she had gained a couple of pounds, there were bags under her eyes. He could tell that she was a victim of drug abuse and only God knew what else. That was the hardest decision that he had to make, and his heart was heavier now than it was when they first ran into the house. Their union had only caused another painful good-bye.

"It's not good-bye," Marie said, reading his mind. She forced a smile to her face. "It's see you soon."

She removed Tyler's hand from her face with the understanding that she was just a small player in a game of blood and war. She wiped her own tears away and Looney smiled at her.

"My nigga," he nodded, respectfully shaking her hand like he would one of his bros.

Marie laughed weakly and Tyler pulled out his cell-phone and charger from his pocket.

"Keep this on silent but check it every five minutes," he instructed her, handing the device to her. "I'll be back in three days."

Marie took the phone and simply nodded her head. She breathed deep and hugged them both one last time.

"See you soon," she whispered and watched them place their masks back over their faces.

With one final wave Tyler unlocked the door with the keys in his hand and walked in front of Looney. Guns drawn, they silently made their exit up the stairs. Tyler refused to look back, because he knew if he did he wouldn't have the nerve to leave his sister there.

Don't look back, Marie thought, knowing her brother like the back of her hand. *Please don't look back*.

When they were out of sight, she shut the door and went to hide the phone under her mattress. There was no doubt in her mind that Tyler would come back to her, but she knew those would be the hardest three days in her life. She sighed loudly and turned on a movie.

"Day one."

Chapter 11

Every hustler would have his day, and that was exactly why Tyreek moved at night. He pushed his cocaine-white Maserati up I-94 toward the Detroit Metro airport, and the sound of Nipsey Hussle flooded the inside of the vehicle. He nodded his head to the lyrics of Nip's song "Overtime" and vibed out to the words of a real nigga. He was running late to get Khiron—the unexpected always happened when you were in a rush. Many thoughts were floating through his mind as he drove, so he barely saw the interstate lights or heard the hard raindrops beating his car.

Tyreek had been Khiron's right hand man for the past five years. When they first met, Khiron was cut throat. He was hungry, but not greedy like the man he had become. His boy had to get it out of the mud in order to make his claim on Atlanta. There was no man there that could hold a candle to Khiron, and if they could it was quickly blown out. He was a boss of his own invention, but everything changed when his connect got bumped up and the streets got dry. Khiron wasn't stupid. As soon as he could he had a meeting set up with who he hoped would be his new connect. That night after that meeting with Ray, Tyreek watched the birth of a man scorned. His anger was uncontrollable, and he wasn't going to stop until he got what he wanted. Tyreek remembered the night he first realized that Khiron would never be the same.

"These muhfuckas get their work from the Italians,"
Khiron spoke in an enraged tone to Tyreek.

Tyreek parked his car on the street behind Khiron's
and hopped in on Khiron's passenger side. Tyreek could
hear the silent rage in his voice when they were on the
phone. He had used his GPS to find the location that
Khiron sent him. Tyreek came up on Khiron posted in the
hood, watching two young cats fucking off with a group
of people on the block. Khiron filled him in on what had
gone down that night, and Tyreek couldn't hide the fact
that he was surprised at the revelation about Mocha.
But then again he wasn't, there was always something
about her that he could never quite put his finger on.

"Damn," he said, shaking his head.

"I'm going to kill all of them," Khiron growled, keeping
his eyes on the prize.

Tyreek looked at the two men Khiron was eyeing.

"Them?" Tyreek asked, nodding toward where the
men stood with laughing faces.

"That's two of 'em," Khiron said, and he watched the
two men dap up their homies and walk back to their
Corvette. "They're just the first to die."

They watched the Corvette start up and began to tail it
when it pulled off, making sure not to get too close. They
didn't drive far before the Corvette stopped and parked
outside of a house in the same neighborhood. Parking
a few houses down, Khiron and Tyreek watched the
men exit the car and walk through the grass to get to
the front door of the house they parked in front of. The
door opened and behind it were two hood rats smiling
from ear to ear at the sight of them. Khiron reached
over Tyreek and opened the glove box. He then handed
Tyreek an all black mask and he put his own on his face.
Tyreek already knew what was up, and Khiron didn't
have to ask if he was down. Tyreek had lost track of his

own body count, so a couple more added didn't make any difference. He didn't stop to think about it. All he knew was that if Khiron had beef with them, then they were the enemy. He was trained to go. They waited for five minutes before Khiron decided it was time to move.

"Come on," Khiron said, and was the first one out of the car.

They moved quickly in the night until they reached the door of the house they'd seen the two niggas disappear in. Guns pointed forward, Tyreek kicked the door in. The house was spotless, and the smell of bleach filled their nostrils. Tyreek heard moans and grunts coming from different rooms. They didn't even hear the door kick in.

"These niggas getting caught slipping for some pussy?" Khiron scoffed and went to the room in the far back of the one story house.

Tyreek went to the one beside it. When he opened the door he saw the baby faced nigga fucking the shit out of a yellow bitch with the fattest ass Tyreek had ever seen. With all the smacking and moaning in the air they didn't hear the small creak of the door opening. But when Tyreek cocked his pistol, it was as if instinct took over for young Baby Face. His ears were trained to the sounds of a gun. Just as Tyreek let out three shots, his target hopped out of the way. The bullets found their home in the head of the big booty bitch; she didn't even know what had hit her.

"What the fuck?" Baby Face said, making a quick grab for his pistol on the nightstand by the bed, but Tyreek already had his gun aimed at him. Baby Face realized he'd gotten got as he stood there naked and unarmed. "Bitch-ass nigga."

Tyreek admired the kid's heart; not once did he beg for his life. That was something Tyreek was used to *hearing from his victims. Instead, he stood there with his head held high. The gold in the pyramid of his Last Kings tattoo glistened on his chest.*

"Do what you gotta do," the kid said shrugging his shoulders.

"It's just business," Tyreek said and emptied his clip into the kid's body.

Tyreek watched his body fall and saw the stream of blood begin to form under his body and onto the carpet. He felt nothing. Like he said, business was business. In the next room he heard gunshots that mimicked his, a scream, and then silence. Within seconds, Khiron was in the room with Tyreek.

"Bitch," he said, coldly spitting on him. "Drag that nigga in the living room."

While Tyreek completed the task, Khiron left the house, saying that he had to grab something from the car. Once he got back in the house he dragged the first victim to the living room. When Tyreek saw what Khiron had gone to grab he just shook his head.

"What you about to do with that, fam?" Tyreek asked, looking at the sharp machete. "The niggas are already dead!"

Khiron responded by kneeling down and examining the ugly young man's face. He looked to be only in his early twenties, and Khiron felt no remorse at all the life he had just stolen from him.

"This is only the beginning," he whispered before he went on hacking off the dead boy's head.

Tyreek didn't agree with how Khiron took Detroit. He didn't feel that there was any honor in it. If the Dominicans weren't backing them Tyreek was sure that the streets would have retaliated because of the death of their king, but instead they just looked with hateful eyes.

Tyreek pulled up to the airport to see his right hand waiting for him. Every hustler had his day, and Khiron? He was a daytime type of nigga.

Chapter 12

Khiron sat in the passenger seat of his boy's car, tired and knowing sleep wouldn't find him any time soon. Khiron didn't feel the need to ask Tyreek why he was late, he figured he was trying to tie up some loose ends. Tyreek was all about his business.

"You drop that shit off to Mocha for Sunday night?" Khiron asked, closing his eyes.

"Yeah, bro," Tyreek nodded his head.

"Good looks," Khiron said. "This is going to be a big move for us, bigger than taking this city. The drug market is changing; old ways to hustle are becoming extinct. The Dominicans have what we need. What they're pitching me is an opportunity that comes with never-ending business. Never-ending money"

"What exactly are they pitching, besides more work?" Tyreek inquired.

"You just said it," Khiron said with his eyes still closed. "More weight means expansion. Keeping business in Atlanta and Detroit is like eating at the same restaurant over and over. More work will allow *us* to be the connect."

"Sounds like they're trying to reinvent The Last Kings bro," Tyreek commented.

"But better," Khiron said, not denying the allegation.

Khiron knew from the beginning that he was just a pawn in a budding war. However, he didn't give a fuck, at the moment he was on the winning side. He'd played a big part in getting the Dominicans to where they were.

He'd single handedly ended The Last Kings operation, and that would forever grant him a pardon with the Dominicans. He did not trust them, but Khiron knew that the golden rule in hustling was that there was no such thing as trust. Trust is what got you killed. All he knew was that meeting with Don Rivera would put the icing on the cake of a never-ending money flow.

Tyreek dropped Khiron off at his home away from home. The neighborhood Khiron chose was a quiet one on the outskirts of Detroit in Bloomfield Hills. It had low crime rate and he didn't have to worry about much there. He kept his location a secret, the only person who knew where his home was located was Tyreek. The neighborhood was quiet and surrounding his large home were others to match.

After he dapped Tyreek up as a farewell he got out of the car and trudged up to his front door. Once inside his Victorian style home, he dropped his suitcase and made his way to the staircase in the dark. He didn't have a live-in maid; he had a service come clean it once a week though. The master bedroom was the size of three regular-sized rooms, and when Khiron flicked on the light switch he saw that everything was where he left it. There were a few papers on his bed and his navy blue slip on house shoes were on the floor beside his bed. He fell into his bed and got comfortable, but it wasn't long before his phone started to ring. He answered as soon as he saw who it was.

"Wassup, mom," he answered the phone.

"Hey, baby!" His mother Alanna's usual, cheery voice greeted him. "What are you up to?"

"You know me, ma," Khiron said, kicking his shoes off and laying back into his plush pillows. "I'm just chilling."

Khiron's mother made it her duty to call her only child every day just to check on him. She knew what life he lived; he was just like his father. Stupid. The streets spoke and he was drawn to them. She knew there wasn't much she could say, after all he was a grown man. He also kept her looking young and living well, so she never even entertained the thought of trying to sway him from his lifestyle anymore. She was a great mother, but she had become a greedy woman—which was the reason Khiron's father had left her, even though it was his fault she had become that way. She was money hungry and didn't know how to get it on her own. She and Khiron's father were together for years, and he had always taken care of her finances. She even dealt with the other women because she knew that even if they were getting his dick they weren't getting what she was getting. He didn't take care of them, nor did he love them. Little did she know, Nino didn't love her either, he was just used to her. He knew that he could trust her with the keys to any safe. But when he met Camara, that all changed. She was the reason Nino ultimately left his already made family. Her foreign features had him hypnotized enough to forget about his family.

Khiron knew what his mother had gone through and he loved her enough to give her the world that his father should have. He felt that she deserved everything he bought her and everything that he did for her. He knew how hard it was raising him by herself. Nino only came around when he wanted to, and his mother fell for it every time. Nino, of course, sent them money, but that still didn't make up for his absence during his son's early childhood. Khiron loved his father, but he could never forgive him for leaving his mother for his side chick. By walking out on her, he had, in a sense, walked out on Khiron.

When Khiron got older Nino started coming around more often, grooming him for the throne as he would call it. Khiron was to take over Nino's empire when it was time. He gave his son work to flip while he went home to play house with his new bitch and her daughter.

"How is everything in Atlanta?" Alanna asked.

"Good," Khiron was brisk with her; he didn't really feel like talking. "Just been handling some business, as usual, you know how it is."

"Sounds like you don't really want to be on the phone," she said matter-of-factly. "I was just calling to check on my one and only baby."

"My bad, ma," he said, knowing his mother was the queen of bitching. "How are things in Baltimore?"

The two continued to make small talk until Khiron convinced her that he really did have to go. Once he was able to finally hang up the phone he put it on the pillow next to him. He listened to the silence of his house and let his eyes stalk the ceiling of his room. Many things had changed in his life. It was like a gold mine had fallen into his lap and he was still trying to pick up all the precious pieces. It was like it kept getting refilled. He was making more money than ever and he pushed more work than he had even seen in a year. His mind fell on what Tyreek had said in the car.

"Sounds like they're trying to reinvent The Last Kings, fam."

Khiron couldn't help but to feel that although he had killed Ray, he had not killed his presence. Whenever he was in the streets of Detroit, he was reminded of him. He understood that they were loyal, but they needed to recognize their new leader. It was his work that kept money flowing in their city. Khiron's thoughts jumped from Ray to Sadie. He wished he could bring her back to life just so he could kill her again. The fact that she and Mocha were so close was the reason he couldn't forgive Mocha. She was directly connected to the ones who were responsible for his father's demise. The fact that she kept her affiliation with The Last Kings a secret let him know that he couldn't trust her. At one point in time, Khiron was in love with Mocha, he was even planning on putting a ring on her finger. Now he couldn't look at her without being disgusted. His anger clouded his judgment, and in that case, he didn't care. He didn't respect her and he showed her that whenever he was in town. Never the less, no matter how unhappy Mocha was, she hadn't taken her own life yet, like he assumed she would. His use of her was almost up, though. He could have any bitch on his arm during a business meeting, but there was something about Mocha's aura that just spoke the language of a *boss*. She could sway any man into doing business with Khiron by just sitting there. He knew he needed her one last time. Once the deal was sealed he had planned to give her what she wanted. A bullet neatly wrapped in the bone of her skull.

Chapter 13

When Tyler walked through the door I was in the middle of cleaning my pistol on the living room couch. He didn't need instructions on how to get to the house because he already knew where it was. I hopped up with the anticipation of seeing Marie alive and well, but when all I saw was Tyler and Looney walk into the living room, I gave them a confused look.

"She wasn't there?" I asked, seeing the stoic expression on Tyler's face when he took a seat beside me on the couch.

I sat my gun on the table in front of me and turned my body to face him. His response was to rub his chin with a nod, without looking at me.

"Well, then what the fuck? Where is she at, in the car? Tell that girl to come on in here!" I asked, looking from him to Looney.

"She stayed, she had to," Tyler said shocking me.

"If she had left that would have been a red flag to that nigga," Looney said, speaking of Khiron. "So she decided to stay. Li'l mama got heart. She's taking one for the team."

It was a sad realization, but I understood. Marie had just earned her respect from me. I reached over and grabbed Tyler's hand.

"When this shit is over we *will* bring her home, I promise," I told him and he just nodded his head. I turned back to Looney. "It's late, so you can sleep here tonight Loon."

"Nahhh," Looney said sarcastically. "Did you think a nigga was gonna drive home? You smoking that shit, Say?"

Despite the situation, Tyler laughed and I did too. Looney was a mood lightener. Once you got past his rough and intimidating outer layer he was actually a joy to be around. At that moment I was thankful for him.

"Shut yo' ass up, nigga," I said, still laughing. "I ain't smoking shit, I was just trying to be hospitable."

"Yeah, yeah," Looney said walking toward the stairs. "I'm going to sleep! I'll see y'all in the morning!"

After he disappeared I turned my attention back to Tyler. I gently put my hand on his soft cheek and pulled myself closer to him. My God, had I missed him, and I knew he needed me right then.

"I shouldn't have left her," Tyler said, looking down at me. "I found her to lose her again? What the fuck am I thinking, Say? She could die tomorrow."

"Shhh," I cooed him like a baby. "Marie is strong, and if she survived for this long she can for a few more days. Her decision was the best one. You didn't lose her. Once we handle business we're going to get her."

"She's in a whore house, Say . . . my baby sister is in a whore house."

His fists clenched tightly shut and I had to admit too that what he had just told me was a big pill to swallow. I didn't know what to say. I knew what went on in those houses, and to my knowledge The Last Kings didn't have one. They treated the women there like cattle, they weren't even considered human most of the time. I knew now why it had been so hard for Tyler to leave her there and why he was reacting in such a way. I didn't know how else to make him feel any better other than to let him let off some frustration . . . inside of me. I kissed him softly on the mouth and let my thumb caress his cheek.

"I love you, Tyler," I said under my breath. "I love you with every piece of me."

The words came out so naturally and harbored so much emotion. Before I knew it, Tyler was kissing me back. Our tongues fondled each other and we shared multiple deep, passionate kisses. It had been so long since I had been with him, and I instantly felt my panties moisten. I moaned into his mouth when I felt his hands begin to explore my body, becoming familiar with it all over again. His fingers pinched my nipples and I flinched at the pleasurable pain. His hands gripped my shirt, and with one great tug he ripped it and my bra away from my body and laid me down on the couch in one swift move. He palmed my breasts and took his time sucking them. The way he kissed and licked them sensually sent electricity from my head to my feet. My toes curled with the intensity of the first orgasm my body released.

"Tyler," I breathed into the air.

His kisses began to go lower and lower until his mouth reached its destination. He gently took off my cotton shorts and moved my lace thong to the side, exposing my fat my treasure. My back arched at the first lick.

"Mmmm," he moaned as his tongue circled faster and faster.

I forgot where I was when I started to scream his name. He slurped up every drop of my sweet nectar that threatened to slide down my thighs. He gripped my thighs and flipped me around so that I could ride his face, which I did without hesitation. While I was riding his face I heard him take off his pants, but I was too focused on my second orgasm to really pay it any mind.

"Oh, Tyler! Mmmm . . . right there, baby," I moaned while he sucked on my clit. "Ty . . . I'm about to—"

I couldn't finish my sentence because he gripped my waist and slid me down to his groin. I felt his thick nine inches slide inside of me, and I instantly released on his shaft. My juices were oozing all over him, and seeing that turned me on even more. I began riding him like a woman who just couldn't get enough of sexing him, because I couldn't. It was even better because he matched me thrust for thrust.

"Sadie . . . fuck, ma!" he moaned and I felt his hands grip my ass tighter, digging deeper into my love box.

He moved his left hand from my ass and began to circle my clit with his thumb, and it caused me to clench my pussy walls tighter around his shaft. I felt my third orgasm coming and I knew he was almost at his peak.

"Fuuuuccckkk!" I screamed as I squirted all over his stomach.

I felt his dick pulsate inside of me, so I quickly hopped off it and replaced my pussy with my mouth. I tasted myself on his dick and I licked it all up hungrily.

"Ahhhh!" he exclaimed in pure ecstasy, gripping my hair tightly as he came inside my mouth.

I gladly drank him all up and didn't stop sucking until I felt him go limp. I wiped my mouth and climbed on top of him. He pulled me down and held me there.

"I love you, ma," he kissed my forehead.

"I know," I said, laying my head on his chest.

I listened to the sound of his heart beat, and as much as I wanted to stay awake and just talk to him, I couldn't. My eyes closed naturally, but for the first time in months I fell asleep happy.

The happy sleep didn't last long. I woke up to a still sound-asleep Tyler. His body felt cold, so I stood up and got a blanket for him to cover up with. Kissing him on his forehead, I made my way upstairs to my bedroom to put some clothes on. Once inside my room I hurriedly went to my drawer and put on some cotton shorts and a tank top. Just as I was on my way back down the stairs I heard my phone vibrating in my purse on the dresser. It was late and I had no idea who would be calling me at that time of night. Looking at the caller ID, it said UNKNOWN.

"Hello?"

"You have mail," I recognized the voice as Vinny's right before he disconnected the call.

Rude ass could have at least said bye, I thought and bounded down the stairs to the front door.

I opened the door, and sure enough on the stoop there was a large folder. I shut the door and ripped into the folder. When I saw what was inside I smiled. I knew the Italians would come through. I was sure not to wake up Tyler as I ran up the stairs to get Adrianna and Devynn. In a matter of five minutes I came up with a plan. It was time to pay Mocha another visit.

Chapter 14

Mocha felt her second phone vibrating from where she kept it hidden under her mattress. It was three in the morning, and she lay on her bed wide awake as she ignored the soft buzz of her mattress. It had been a while since Mocha had gone on a date. Her clients had been blowing her phone up, but she didn't feel the need to entertain them anymore.

Strangely, her thoughts fell to Tyreek. She wanted to warn him so badly about what was coming, but as fucked up and twisted as it seemed . . . she couldn't. She was just about to turn on her side to try and get some rest, but in the silence of her home she heard the jangling of her doorknob being tampered with. Before she could get up and go see who it was she heard the door open and close. Without thinking, Mocha reached under her mattress and pulled out her chrome weapon. She hopped out of the bed with a killer mentality and held the gun steadily in front of her. She knew not to say, "Who is it?" Only bimbo bitches did that in movies; she wanted her attacker to be caught off guard. She moved silently into her hallway, protected by the darkness of her home. When she got to the entrance of the living room she turned with her gun extended to see a small, dark figure standing before her. Without hesitation, she pulled the trigger. When nothing happened she pulled again . . . and again. Still nothing.

"You should know better than to hide your gun under your mattress, Mo," Mocha heard a familiar female voice say.

Suddenly the lights were flicked on and she was able to see who her intruders were. Sitting on the couches in her tiny living room were two faces she hadn't seen in over a year. Devynn and Adrianna stared back at Mocha with nothing but resentment in their eyes. Standing in front of her was Sadie. They were dressed in all black; Mocha assumed that was to be undetected in the hood. She knew Khiron's dogs were watching her house. All three women wore black hoodies, black jean shorts, with all-black low top Chuck Taylor's. Sadie turned her palms and let go of what she was holding in her hands. Whatever it was made of it made a loud pitter-patter on Mocha's wooden floor. Looking down, Mocha saw that they were the bullets to her unloaded gun.

"You've lost your touch, Mo," Sadie commented. "You can't even tell the difference between a loaded and unloaded gun."

Mocha threw the gun down and shrugged her shoulders at Sadie; she didn't know what she was supposed to say. She stood there, unarmed, in nothing but a black Victoria's Secret teddy with lace boy short underwear.

"Sit," Devynn instructed from the brown couch and nodded to the black love seat across from where she and Adrianna sat.

Mocha looked at Sadie before she moved.

"Bitch, I'm not going to shoot you when your back is turned. I'm not you," Sadie snapped. "Go sit down, we have business to talk about and we don't have much time. The tranquilizers we shot your man's goons with will stop working in an hour."

Her comment stung, but Mocha obliged and sat on the love seat by herself. Sadie joined Adrianna and Devynn across from her. She got comfortable between them.

"Damn, Mo, this nigga got you living like a fuckin' slave," Devynn said, shaking her head as she glanced around the place Mocha called home. "You don't even have matching furniture! Hell, nah."

Adrianna stifled a laugh.

"Shut up, Dev," she said.

As they made fun of her, Mocha realized how much she missed them. They were like her sisters. But she knew no amount of apologizing would make them forgive her. Despite the sweet outside layer she knew they had, deep inside they were ruthless killers, and she had gotten on their bad sides. Adrianna laid a big, slightly bulky manila folder on the table that separated them.

"Open it," Sadie informed her, but Mocha was already reaching for the folder.

She opened the folder and pulled out what seemed to be a big blueprint sheet. When she looked closer at it she saw that it *was* a blueprint sheet. The question was, of what, though? Her suspense didn't drag out for long.

"That's the blueprint of the hotel that Khiron will be meeting Don Rivera in," Sadie said bluntly.

Mocha looked to her and couldn't help but to wonder how she came across the information. She didn't even know where the meeting would be held. But not only did Sadie know, she had a paper that listed every single room inside of the building with tacks stuck to it, telling you which room was which.

"Even with the Dominicans running Detroit the Italians still have reach here, Mo. An informant told our Italian connect of the location."

"The Italians are here?" Mocha asked, trying to disguise the anxious tone in her voice.

It didn't go unnoticed by the women before her, and they all gave her a knowing look.

"Nobody is going to touch you before the meeting, Mocha," Sadie said, and Mocha took heed.

"Why?" Mocha asked.

"Didn't I tell you that we need you?" Sadie said.

"You never said for what, though," Mocha snapped back and glared at her.

"We know the building that Khiron is meeting Don Rivera in," Sadie started. "But we don't know what room. We can assume that the meeting will last all of fifteen minutes—that isn't enough time to play Guess What Room. That's where you come in at."

"How am I supposed to tell you what room it will be in? They wouldn't even tell me where the meeting is, let alone give me access to a phone to—" Mocha stopped when she saw what Adrianna pulled from behind her.

In Adrianna's hands was a small device the size of half a pinky fingernail, a needle and stitches, a towel, and a sharp knife. When Sadie saw Mocha's confused face, she smiled.

"It's a tracking device. Adrianna is going to put it in your arm," Sadie informed her. When she saw Mocha open her mouth to protest she made her voice turn cold and held up her hand. "Shut the fuck up. You don't have a choice. Do it, A."

Adrianna got up from her seat next to Sadie and went and took a seat next to Mocha. The sleeveless teddy was perfect for the procedure Adrianna was about to perform on the back of Mocha's shoulder.

"Don't worry, Mo," Adrianna said with a slick smile. "This will be very painful."

Mocha heard Devynn laugh, and before she could brace herself she felt searing pain at the back of her left shoulder.

"Shit!" Mocha screamed with her eyes clenched shut.

Squeezing the couch cushion while biting her lip, she managed to open her eyes to glance at Sadie and saw her watching with a pleased expression plastered across her face. She was enjoying Mocha's discomfort. Once Adrianna had successfully planted the device into Mocha's shoulder she stitched her up and wiped away any access blood.

"All done," Adrianna said, standing up.

Sadie and Devynn stood up as well. The three of them walked toward the door.

"We'll be seeing you," Sadie said and flicked off Mocha's living room light before she shut the door behind her.

Mocha didn't move from the couch right away, she just sat there in the dark. She knew now that Sadie would be watching her every move. She didn't know if that was a good thing or bad thing. In less than two days everything would either change for the worse, or go back to normal. Mocha knew she was just a pawn in the game. If things would have been different, she would have been a soldier fighting with her sisters instead of a pawn. But then again, if things were different there wouldn't even be a war to fight. Ray would be alive and The Last Kings would still be on top.

Mocha finally stood up from the couch and walked slowly back to her room. On her way up, her foot kicked something and stubbed her pinky toe.

"Fuck," she whispered, wincing at the pain.

She turned on the hallway light to see what had caused her pain. She looked down and saw that it was her gun that she had thrown down. Bending down, she grabbed it and snatched up all the bullets around it. When she held the gun that time she did notice that it was a little lighter, she didn't know how she didn't feel it earlier. She got back to her room and placed her gun back into its hiding spot so that she could lay back down in her bed.

The throbbing and discomfort in her shoulder caused her to have to sleep on her right side. Sadie was right, she had lost her touch. Although a small part of her missed the life she lived as a hustler, she knew she wouldn't ever go back to it. Things would never be the same; she would always be looked at the same way people looked at snitches. No one that mattered would give her respect despite the affiliation she once had.

She knew by the way Sadie looked at her when she sat there cringing in pain what her intentions were after her use for Mocha was up in less than two days. But at that moment, she decided that she wasn't ready to die. She wasn't going to just *let* anyone kill her. Mocha would miss Tyreek. Over the past year she had grown a strange attachment to him, but she also knew that she had to get far away from anybody she knew. She had enough of her own money saved up to make the trip and to live off of until she found a job.

"Brazil sounds nice," she said, right before sleep found her.

Chapter 15

Devynn stood in the doorway of Sadie's room and watched her sleeping soundly on her bed. She leaned on the door frame and watched as Sadie's chest heaved up and down. Devynn viewed Sadie like a little sister, and she knew how much she and Adrianna were needed. The weight of the world had fallen on that girl's shoulders, and Devynn didn't know how she could even sleep at all. She felt somebody come from up behind her, but she did not avert her eyes.

"She's beautiful," Devynn heard Adrianna's voice say.

Devynn didn't respond. She finally stepped back and walked down the hallway to the big room that she and Adrianna had began sharing since the arrival of Tyler and Looney. She walked to the dresser and pulled out a fifth of scotch and two glasses from the top drawer.

"What's wrong, mami?" Adrianna followed her back to the room

It was obvious something was bothering Devynn, and she didn't need to see the glasses of scotch being poured to realize that. Devynn took a long gulp of the drink and welcomed the burning sensation trickling down her throat. She took another before she turned back to Adrianna, handing her a glass.

"I don't want to fail again," Devynn said, shaking her head. "I-"

She paused and clenched her glass in her left hand. Devynn wasn't a crier, but her thoughts caused a glaze to come over her eyes. She took a brisk breath and pursed her lips tightly together.

"You what, boo?" Adrianna said, urging her friend to continue. "What's on your mind, Dev?"

"I can't lose another one of y'all," Devynn swallowed. "After D and Amann . . . Ray. I just can't. I feel like I have to be strong for Say, but this shit has been wearing tough on my heart."

Adrianna stood still, shocked. Devynn had always been the fearless one of the twosome. Although Adrianna wanted to comfort her with words, she knew there was no promise that she could make to reassure Devynn that everything would turn out okay. You couldn't make those kinds of promises in a war. Sadie wouldn't tell anybody what was going on in that head of hers, but Adrianna knew that they had to trust her.

"All we can do is trust her, Dev," Adrianna said, setting her cup down without even taking a sip. "In every war there will be casualties, you know that. Put that glass down, mami, we need clear heads. The next drink we have will be to celebrate The Last Kings taking back what's ours."

"I know," Devynn said as she put her almost emptied glass back down on the dresser. She went and sat on her queen-sized bed and looked deeply into Adrianna's eyes. "I never thought any of this shit would happen, man. Seeing Mocha face-to-face just brought all this pain back. Some nights I can't sleep because I can't get the images of my bros out of my head."

"I know," Adrianna agreed. She took a seat beside Devynn and placed her arm around her shoulder. "I almost slit that bitch's throat, but we need her for now. We have to play our cards the way they were dealt. When the time comes, Mocha will pay for all that she has done."

"You think Say is going to be able to do it, though? You think she'll be able to kill Mocha?" Devynn asked.

Adrianna wanted to answer the question, but in all honesty she didn't know. Granted, Mocha deserved to die for everything that had gone down. Adrianna also knew that Sadie's heart wasn't completely black. Although she had hate in her heart for Mocha, Adrianna also knew love was still there as well. Mocha was a reminder to Sadie of who she once was.

"Well," Devynn continued when Adrianna didn't comment, "If she can't pull the fuckin' trigger, trust and believe I will. That bitch needs to be in the dirt. The fact that we still share the same air disgusts me. That bitch has to die."

What Devynn said was meant wholeheartedly. The image of Ray's flesh being eaten by the acid flooded her mind. There was no way that Mocha could walk after that. The days Khiron gave her were a blessing and a half, because that was as much leniency as she would be granted. She and Adrianna sat in silence, but they were both thinking the same thing. They couldn't wait until the morning came. Everybody would finally touch down in Detroit, and final plans could be put into place. Vinny was supposed to show his face as well, but knowing Vinny, he was probably already there watching all of them.

"Let's go get something to eat," Adrianna finally said, removing her arm. "We need to put something in our stomachs."

She didn't wait for Devynn to answer before she grabbed her purse and started toward the bedroom door. She was hungry, but the last thing she wanted to do was go into the kitchen to cook. Her stomach was yearning for something greasy and that wouldn't be good for her figure. She didn't hear Devynn behind her as she made her way through the house down to the front door. She heard voices when she passed the entrance to the living room. She smirked when she heard Looney and Tyler shit talking about whatever game they were watching and decided not to intrude to tell them where she was going. Once she got to the front door her girl appeared beside her.

"I thought you might change your mind," she said, winking once they got outside.

"Shut up," Devynn said, walking to the side of the house where Adrianna's new gold Audi A8 was parked. "You better not take me anywhere that serves bullshit, A."

Adrianna didn't even entertain her comment when she got in the driver's seat. All For One served not one nasty dish, so she knew Devynn wouldn't be disappointed. It was a restaurant that she frequented with Ray and it had the best food that she had ever tasted. She hadn't gone since they'd been back in Detroit, and she hoped that the memories weren't too much for her to bear. She didn't speak on her personal feelings for Ray simply because she knew the pain that she felt was nothing compared to Sadie's, but still, the love she had for that man was so transparent. Out of all the men from her past, he had been the only one to feed her mind and give her soul a heartbeat. She cocked her head as she whizzed through the night traffic and both women sung along to Fetty Wap's voice.

"You are so damn fine, I'm so damn glad you're mine! Aye! And you stay on my mind, I think about you all the damn time!"

It took a little over half an hour to get to the restaurant, and once there it was clear to see that All For One was a hot commodity at that time of night. It was the only restaurant in the neighborhood that stayed open later than midnight. Both Devynn and Adrianna stepped out of the vehicle, dressed casually in shorts and T-shirts. The concrete under their feet was blessed with each step they took in their barely worn sneakers. Once inside, they were seated at a booth in a far right corner. The aroma in the air coming from the kitchen was like heaven, and the restaurant was loud with good vibes. Most of the people sitting around them were dressed to the nines like they had just come from the club.

"This a hood spot," Devynn observed with raised eyebrows after they placed their orders.

Adrianna's eyes traveled around the restaurant and fell on all the young faces there. She didn't need to be a rocket scientist to see that the group of young men sitting around the table to the far left were corner boys. The guns on a few of their waists bulged through their shirts, and the ice on their wrists shined like there was no tomorrow. The gold in their teeth and around their necks signified that they were getting some kind of money.

"Fuck them," Adrianna said, already knowing that they had to work for Khiron.

"You think it's smart for us to be out in the open like this?" Devynn asked when the waitress finally brought their food out to them.

"What's the worst that can happen?" Adrianna asked, popping a salty fry in her mouth.

She definitely spoke too soon. Unknown to them, there were a set of eyes on them straining to figure out why the two sexiest women in the restaurant looked so familiar. In that same booth in the far left corner, a young hustler by the name of Taylor, Tay for short, had been eyeing the two women since they had walked in. He was a built, light-skinned man with a full beard. He wore an oversized shirt and a pair of deep blue Levis with money knots in the pockets.

"I know you ain't staring at them hoes when you got me on ya lap, nigga!" Carmen, the woman Tay had been planning to smash all night, said, leaning in his face and blocking his view. It was true, she was a bad piece, but his focus was completely thrown off.

"Man, who the fuck are you talking to?" Tay said and pushed her off his lap. "You ain't shit but some pussy. What? You thought you was special?"

At that moment, one of the women stood up, and he got a good look at her thigh. It felt like time around him stopped. The Last King tattoo was plain as day, and he knew exactly where he remembered her from. Tay had been with Khiron when he ran up into Ray's house. He had also been the one to put the slug into that girl Sadie's chest.

"Nigga, you got me fucked up!" Carmen's voice started to escalate, but her friends calmed her down before she could get too loud.

"Bitch, if you don't shut your drunk ass up! These niggas don't play that acting a fool mess, they got guns and shit!"

Tay ignored the whores around the table, instead he waited for the woman to come back from the restroom. Once she was seated, he leaned in to a few of the other runners around and whispered something to them. He then nodded his head toward the table with the women and they understood the threat.

"I thought Khiron had them hoes killed?" One of them asked Tay.

"Clearly not," Tay said, placing his hand on the gun at his waist. "But the way I see it, this is a way to climb in ranks boys. We gon' handle these bitches tonight and take their heads to Khiron when we're done."

The men subtly watched the women until they finally paid their bill, leaving a hundred dollar tip apiece, and got up to leave.

"All right, let's move out," Tay said. "You bitches stay here."

"Bitches? And you think you getting some of *this* pussy?"

"Carmen, shut the fuck up! I need my phone bill paid! You tripping!" another one of the girls exclaimed.

Paying them no mind, Tay, followed by the other three men, casually walked out of the restaurant. As soon as the night air hit them, they had their guns drawn.

"I thought I seen them walking toward that Audi right there," one of them, Lee, said.

However, the gold Audi was still parked with no one in it. Tay looked around and smacked his lips as he pulled up his sagging Levis.

"Where these bitches go, man? Khiron gon' flip shits when he finds out we seen these hoes and didn't kill 'em!"

"Fuck that nigga!" a voice called in the distance right before gunshots rang out in the parking lot.

The men were sitting ducks. They had walked right into Devynn and Adrianna's trap. Instantly, two of the four men dropped, while the other ones tried to jump for cover. That didn't do them any good though, especially since they didn't know where their enemy was firing from. The men thought they were being discreet the whole time they were scoping the women out, however it wasn't Adrianna's first time around the rodeo. As soon as Devynn left to go to the restroom she noticed the spark in one of the hustler's eyes. It was the look of a man who had just come up on a plug. She then noticed Devynn's tattoo showing and instantly put two and two together. When they walked out of the building together she briefed Devynn on what she thought was about to happen, so the two split up. Sure enough, they were followed out the door, and they both knew what had to be done.

"Fire back, pussy-ass nigga," Devynn said and ran up on one of the men hiding behind a Suburban.

She had literally come out of nowhere, and he didn't have time to react before her right fist connected with his jaw. When he fell backward, she raised her pistol and made it bark. The back of his head instantly blew away, and the concrete under him was painted red.

"Too late now," Devynn said, ducking low. "One more to go."

She peeked around the truck and saw that people in the restaurant were ducking under their tables because of the sound of the gunfire. She wanted Adrianna to hurry up and kill the last nigga so they could hurry up and get out of there; she was sure somebody had called the police.

On the other side of the parking lot, Adrianna was in an all out gun war with Tay.

"Bitch, I can't wait to tell Khiron The Last Kings are back in his city! He's going to gut you mothafuckas alive! Then Tay is going to be the last king!"

"*His* city?" Adrianna said and got on her back to roll under the shot up Cadillac she was hiding behind.

She did so just in time, because Tay stepped around the vehicle and fired his gun.

"You missed!" Adrianna aimed her pistol and squeezed the trigger twice, catching the heavy set man in both of his ankles.

"Ahhh!" he yelled and dropped painfully to the ground.

When Adrianna rolled from underneath the car she hurried to her feet so she could kick Tay's gun far away.

"Kings don't die, motherfucker!" she said before she put two slugs in his face.

"C'mon, A!" Devynn yelled from across the parking lot. "We gotta go!"

Adrianna didn't need to be told twice, and ran to where they had dropped their bags. Swooping them up, she threw Devynn's purse to her and dug into her own so that she could find her keys.

"What about the cameras?" Devynn asked, nodding toward the four dead bodies spread along the now bloody parking lot.

Adrianna clicked the button to unlock the car doors and shook her head.

"Ray used to do so much business here, those things don't work! Come on!"

Adrianna pulled off from the restaurant, burning rubber, and drove like a mad woman back to the direction of the house. Her adrenaline was pumping, and she had to admit, it wasn't in a bad way. It had been so long since she had used her gun that she was almost positive cobwebs were growing on her bullets. Tay's words added more fuel to the fire of her heart; they had to reclaim Detroit. Khiron had these little niggas parading around like they were really somebody.

"I gotta pull over and switch these plates real quick," she told Devynn, coming to a stop on the side of the road and popped her trunk. "I don't know if anybody in the restaurant got my shit. Especially with those loud girls in there."

"Okay," Devynn nodded, looking down at the blood spots on her shirt. "A? What we gon' tell Sadie?"

"Easy," Adrianna said before she stepped out of the vehicle. "We don't."

"Sir, the helicopter is ready," the high pitched voice of a young woman filled the air.

Don Rivera stood in the doorway of the patio at his 15,000 square feet estate as he looked on to the helicopter that would take him to his private jet. Don was a very handsome older man. Although in his midfifties, there were no wrinkles on his face and only a few grays in his dark brown hair. It was safe to say he had aged very well. He stood there, suave in an Ermenegildo Zegna all-black suit, and his brown eyes watched the young beautiful Dominican woman walk away from the helicopter and toward him. Her hair blew wildly in the wind from the propellers, and her pink dress threatened to rise, exposing her secrets beneath. Don barely took notice of it; he had already enjoyed the sweet goodness between her thighs the night before.

"Thank you, Rachel," Don said to her with a small smile on his thin lips.

Don and his black suits walked past her into his large backyard and toward the loud helicopter. Although they would not be taking the trip with him, they knew to be by his side no matter how short of a distance he had to walk. Once at the steps of the helicopter he turned back to the house and saw Rachel standing there, waving good-bye with a big smile on her face.

She was in heaven; all her dreams had come true. Although she was much younger than Don she was almost certain that she loved him, and if not him, she was for certain in love with his money. She met him on a random night on the town and the two of them had been seeing each other for a few weeks. She knew that Don would make sure she was taken care of and her family would finally be able to live well. The expression on her face spoke volumes of happiness. She couldn't wait for Don to leave just so he could hurry back home to take her shopping for more summer dresses.

Don waved back to her before he motioned to one of the Dominican men to come forward. There was only one woman that would ever hold Don's heart, and they had parted years prior. Nobody could ever or would ever replace her in his eyes, no matter how hard she tried. When the man was directly in front of Don's face, Don looked him in his eyes, giving him a message the young man understood completely before Don could even speak.

"Kill her, and make sure he's on the next flight out," Don said, right before he got into the helicopter and the door was shut behind him.

***

The sound of fire crackling and the smell of burning wood evaded the air of an elegant Detroit home. Vinny sat in the living room of his house he hadn't visited since the last time he saw Ray alive. Nobody knew of this home except him and a few of his most trusted accomplices. Vinny had a house in almost every state, simply because he moved around entirely too much to have one main home. They were all decorated with taste, but all different from each other, except the master bedroom. His bedroom in every home, despite the size, was decorated the exact same way. All black furniture, a king-sized bed centered against the wall, and a seventy-inch television hanging directly on the wall in front of him. On the wall above his bed was a painting; the Mona Lisa as a reminder of his heritage.

He sat, staring into the fireplace, lost in his own weary thoughts. He didn't know how badly losing The Last Kings operation would hurt him until it happened. He anticipated somebody eventually coming for his protégé, but he never thought they would be able to knock him off of his throne. Vinny invested in Ray without asking for anything in return but loyalty. He made so much money off of Ray he didn't need to conduct business with anybody else if he didn't want to. And he didn't want to. Vinny was pleased to hear that Sadie wanted to bring the cartel back to life and was more than willing to provide the ammunition and man power to help her. He knew that they were about to fire the second shots in the war. The first shot was when the Dominicans decided to give Khiron their work and assist him in taking over every spot in Detroit. The blatant disrespect was something Vinny would not tolerate. Vinny never felt the need to cut Don Rivera in on his dealings with The Last Kings because *he* was their connect, no need to add more hands in the pot. It was a selfish move on his part, but if the shoe was on the other foot he was almost certain that Don would do the exact same thing.

Being the plug was all that Vinny had to do when Ray was alive. Everything else, Ray did by himself. It was his genius that birthed The Last Kings; Vinny could not even feel entitled if he wanted to. It was Ray that kept money in all of their pockets.

"If I want to stay wealthy, then I have to make sure the people around me are rich."

And that was exactly what he did. The way Vinny felt was that if Don wanted to get in on the business trade with The Last Kings then his place was to go directly to Ray. If Ray decided to cut Don Rivera in, then it wasn't Vinny's place as a man to be angered. Still, it was comforting to know that Ray would never do something like that, his loyalty to Vinny was too strong. The fact that Don would start a war behind a man who used a woman to do his dirty work was the only thing that had Vinny's mind boggled. Either Don's grip on the game was loosening or there was something bigger that Vinny was missing.

Vinny could only guess what the Dominicans had in their plans. He had known Don for years, and he knew what the supreme vision was. Don Rivera's dream was to create the super cartel; one big cartel that controlled numerous cities. He wanted his work to spread like a virus so that no matter what happened there would be a never-ending money flow. However, he never could get it right. The world was too hungry and selfish to come together, for him anyways. Without even trying to achieve that, Vinny swept his dream from right under Don's feet and made it his own reality.

Unknown to the Dominicans, Vinny still held a lot of cards in Detroit. Like the fact that he was still able to enter the city without being detected and he never needed a disguise. His name held weight and he had many ears planted in Detroit. Vinny knew everyone involved in Khiron's operation, all the way down to the names and addressed of the little runners he had working the corners. When your money was tall it didn't take much to get a background check on anybody. He used this knowledge to find out where the meeting between Khiron and Don would be held. Not only that, but he also got the blue prints to the whole building within thirty minutes. All Sadie had to do was get her hands on them and it would be a done deal. When it came down to doing what needed to be done she was thorough, much like her big cousin.

Chapter 16

It had been too long since my last conversation with Legacy, and I was happy to see him walk through the doors of my house Sunday morning. He was the only one who was able to keep me level headed. The closer we got to the day of the meeting the more unsure I became. I was holding a lot of weight on my shoulders, and until then I never really thought about the aftermath. If everything went as planned, then I would rightfully claim my throne as the leader of The Last Kings. Even though Ray and Legacy believed in me I often questioned myself. I knew that no matter how hard I tried, I would never be Ray. I felt that by taking his crown I would only be walking in his shadow. That wasn't what I wanted. I wanted to make my own way and walk the footsteps of my own path. The catch twenty-two was that I didn't know how. When Ray was in charge he ran things smoothly like it was nothing to him. Being a boss came naturally to him. But me? It was true that I was used to people following me, but I always had Ray to leave the trail of bread crumbs. When he was alive I looked up to him figuratively, now I had to literally look up to him; but physically he wasn't there to guide me.

"I would ask how the trip here was," I started grinning up at Legacy. "But that is the least of my interests right now. You are all here in one piece, and that is all that matters. Come on, we're all in the dining room."

Legacy, Lace, Ghost, and Smoke set their bags on the ground so that they could follow behind me. They must have learned from the last meeting because they all introduced themselves. I noticed Lace looking uneasily at me and I saw the bullet wound on her arm had healed quite nicely. I let everyone sit down first before I took my seat at the head of the table. It was time to inform everyone of the plan in my head.

"Don Rivera is either on his way here, or he's already here," I started. "Either way, this is the only real chance we have to get all of this together. We have the blueprints of the whole building that Khiron and Don Rivera will be in, and we have a tracking device in Mocha that will show us exactly where they are in the building."

I paused and looked at everybody's faces. They were all staring intently at me, and I continued.

"This isn't going to just be a run in, pow pow, and the job is done. It sounds easier than it will be. The Dominicans aren't stupid, and in their country they are above the law. Their cartel is powerful. Foul play is to be expected, because much like us, they just don't give a fuck. Don Rivera is going to have the place swarming, so getting to wherever he is will not be like walking into a candy store."

I was prepping them for a real war. It wasn't like a typical street war with just guns and shit. Ray had once told me about the first war between the Italians and the Dominicans. It ended in a stale mate after two blocks were blown up. These people weren't for play-play, they were the real thing.

"Where will the Italians be?" Smoke asked. "You said we had powerful allies."

"They will be there waiting for my signal," I answered. "They can't show their faces too soon, otherwise our window of opportunity will be lost. Don Rivera can't feel that there is a set up happening at all. Not one Italian face will be seen until he feels comfortable in his setting."

They all nodded their understanding.

"I planted a tracking device inside of Mocha just in case I am wrong, but I have a feeling I know where they will be meeting at."

"Where?" Legacy asked me from where he sat next to Lace.

"The rooftop," I answered.

"Why the rooftop?"

I paused for a second and slowly rotated my head to all of the awaiting eyes. I nodded my head slightly, knowing that they were waiting to hear how and why I was so sure.

"Because that's where I would meet at. So Smoke and Ghost, I'm going to have you two positioned on top of buildings around the hotel with a few of our Italian friends. You will be our snipers. Adrianna and Devynn, you will be disguised as maids; you two will be our eyes and ears. The rest of you will be with me. We're the shooters. I just have one request: Khiron is mine. Period."

Everybody, including Lace, nodded their heads. The rest of the day we finished prepping and got all of our weapons ready. It didn't dawn on me until almost six o'clock what was about to happen, but I stopped any negative thought from taking over my mental and I got dressed. Once I was fully dressed I went down to the artillery room to get some extra clips just in case. I heard voices, and upon realizing they belonged to Legacy and Lace, I slowed my pace until I reached a complete stop. I normally didn't eavesdrop on conversations, but when I heard my name I just couldn't help myself.

"You trust her?" I heard Lace ask.

"With my life," Legacy responded.

"Why?"

There was a pause.

C.N. Phillips

"The same reason I trust you with my life," was his response. "She doesn't know how not to be loyal. Her eyes don't lie."

"Do you love her?" Lace's voice was meek and uncertain.

"Like a sister," Legacy said, and there was a noise like he had just set down his gun. "Come on, ma. You know you the only one for me. Come here. The relationship that Sadie and I have is a close one, but it is strictly platonic. Even she recognizes the love that I have for you, but you can't see it?"

"I just have never seen you this way with another woman, Legacy . . . and you let her shoot me."

"Listen, ma. To you, Sadie might be a woman. But to me, she is a nigga—a nigga to be respected at that. We all gotta learn our lesson in the game somehow," Legacy chuckled.

I heard her give a small laugh, and that surprised me.

"Yea, she got my respect after that shit," Lace said.

"I love you, Lace."

I didn't need to hear the wet kiss to know what was about to happen in that room. I just hoped they didn't fuck on top of the grenades and blow us all up. I smiled knowing that Legacy trusted me with his life, and I was shocked at Lace's question. I never pegged her as the insecure type, but I guess if I saw a woman as close to Tyler as I was to Legacy, I would have some questions as well. When I heard a low moan from Lace's mouth I knew it was time to make my exit. I could grab what I needed before we left; they needed that moment of peace. Walking back up the stairs I noticed Ghost coming down them. I grabbed his arm quickly and shook my head.

"Your man is handling some business down there," I smirked.

"Again?" Ghost exclaimed.

I laughed.

"Come on," I said, leading him back up the stairs.

We reached the top of the stairs and saw Devynn making her way toward us.

"Fifteen minutes," I told her and shut the basement door.

If Legacy had been anybody else I would have been cock blocking like a muhfucka, but he was my nigga, and I was letting him do his thing before we set out. I sat with everybody in the living room and we all were talking and joking even though we knew it might be the last day we saw each other alive. That just wasn't a good topic of discussion. After about fifteen minutes, Legacy and Lace showed their faces. We all gave them knowing looks, and they burst out laughing.

"The fuck are y'all looking at?" Lace fake glared at us. "This might be my last day here, shit. A bitch can't get some dick? Sadie, I don't know why you and Tyler haven't snuck off yet."

I rolled my eyes. Little did she know, Tyler had already broken me off for the day. He smiled at me from the couch he was sitting on and I winked back at him.

"Ooooo!" Devynn giggled like a school girl seeing our little exchange. "Y'all nasty!"

"Devynn . . . I know you aren't talking with all that noise you and Smoke were making last night," Adrianna laughed. "Tell me, is he still your daddy?"

Devynn sat looking dumbfounded and everybody else burst out laughing. I saw Tyler and Ghost dap Smoke up. Devynn rolled her eyes.

"Fuck all y'all," she said, trying to hide the smile forming on her face.

Legacy went into the kitchen and came back with a fifth of Hennessey and a shot glass for each of us. He poured us all a shot and set the fifth down. He held his glass in the air. We all stood up and did the same.

"Let's toast to us. If we don't all make it back today, I want you to know I love all of you," he said.

Although he only said two short sentences, his words meant more than even he knew. He was acknowledging the fact that even he may not make it back alive, but that he was still willing to put his life on the line for The Last Kings. The loyalty we had all instilled in each other in such a short amount of time was felt throughout the room. Lace looked to me and smiled, nodding her head approvingly. She lowered her glass and then raised it up to me; to my surprise everyone else did the same. They were waiting for me to speak, so I raised my glass to them and looked each of them in their eyes before taking a breath and saying exactly what they needed to hear.

"To us . . . Kings forever!"

Chapter 17

Mocha stood in the foyer of Khiron's home, waiting for him to come from upstairs. He had his driver go and pick her up that morning so that he could take her out for lunch. Mocha was completely thrown off by the gesture but agreed to join him. She didn't have much say. She wore a long, light blue maxi dress with a big tan hat on her head. She wondered if he was being nice to her because of what was going down that night. Either way, she was on edge. She watched him come down the stairs looking very suave in a V-Neck silk shirt and Burberry shorts that stopped just below his knees. The Burberry aviator glasses and Burberry washed check trainer shoes complimented his outfit nicely, but Mocha would never tell him that. Fuck him. When he reached the end of the stairs he linked arms with Mocha, and that caught her completely off guard. It was something that they once did when they were an actual couple. Instinctively, Mocha removed her arm from his.

"Chill, Mo," Khiron said, smiling at her, and linked their arms together again.

Once again, she was dumbfounded. He hadn't called her "Mo" in forever. Something told her to keep her guard up, because things weren't sitting right with her. Together they exited the house, and Mocha stopped in her tracks when she saw the limousine parked in front of his home. She looked startled at him and her face read pure confusion.

This nigga must've smoked something, Mocha thought to herself. *Either that or he wants something. Damn, I knew I shouldn't have left my gun at the house.*

"Are you about to kill me?" Mocha asked him bluntly.

Khiron laughed loudly.

"No," Khiron answered truthfully.

Not now, anyway, Khiron thought to himself.

At one point in time Mocha had been his lady, and although she kept many secrets from him, to the best of his knowledge she had been faithful sexually. For that, he thought it would be nice of him to at least make her last day on earth a pleasant one. The driver held the door to the back of the limo open and Khiron nodded for her to get in first. Mocha sat to the far window, hoping that he wouldn't scoot too close to her, which of course was exactly what he did. She tried to control the uneasy feeling in her stomach and keep her face as blank as possible. Something wasn't right. She would be a complete fool to believe that the man who had treated her like less than shit suddenly had a change of heart. It was suspect, but for now Mocha went along with it. If anything happened she was mentally prepared to run and scream bloody murder.

"Where are we going?" Mocha asked.

"You'll see," Khiron said, smiling at her.

This nigga is on some funny shit for real, Mocha thought to herself.

She felt like he was trying to catch her slipping. He said he wasn't going to kill her, but the eyes don't lie. Although his face smiled his eyes were a dead giveaway of the hate he harbored for her. She swallowed and turned her head so that she could look out the window, focusing on the scenery that whizzed past.

Khiron stared at her. There was no doubt that she was beautiful and he wouldn't be able to call himself real if he denied the fact that he had once felt love for the woman.

The fact remained that to current day he still loved her, and that was the reason he hated her so. Even when he tried to stop loving her he couldn't; she was his heart. He told her the reason why he didn't kill her was because she was his trophy piece, and that was true to a certain extent. The full truth of the matter was that he couldn't kill her, because by doing so he'd be killing a part of himself. He couldn't be in the same vicinity as her for more than a few hours, and that was why he didn't house her in his own home. He knew that she had the power to bring him back from the dark that he'd grown so accustomed to. He couldn't risk that, especially after what happened the last time he let her in. So he kept her locked away. Nobody else could ever have her. He took her in as a whole. From her perfectly arched eyebrows, to her full lips, all the way down to her breasts, thighs, and manicured toes. She was perfect.

Why did you have to do me like this, shawty? Khiron thought to himself. *Why did you have to be a part of The Last Kings?*

He loved her, but he would never be able to forgive her. He said he was going to kill her after the meeting was done, but he knew he was going to have to hand the gun to one of his goons to complete the deed.

Mocha turned her head and saw Khiron watching her and she felt herself blush. She hated the fact that the man that had become her devil was giving her butterflies.

He beat you, Mocha! She screamed at herself in her head. *He makes you fuck him. He treats you like shit. Don't do that.*

Mocha rolled her eyes at him and flinched hard when she saw his arm move. Expecting to feel a sharp pain as he smacked her face for being disrespectful, she grimaced.

"Chill," Khiron said, pulling his cell phone from his pocket. "I'm not on that right now. We cool."

Mocha was amazed. Any other time he would have floored her and beat her relentlessly. Mocha felt the limo slow down, and looking out the window she saw that they had reached a park. She noticed a picnic setting under a tree that provided tons of shade and she felt herself smile.

"You remember our first real date?" Khiron asked, taking Mocha's hand.

He was supposed to be putting on an act of kindness, but as the time progressed he felt it becoming more and more genuine. He only abused her to release the pain that she had caused him. But most times it ended up hurting him more than it hurt her.

"Yea," Mocha laughed. "That's the day you set up a picnic for us and tried to cook the damn food yourself."

"Chef Khy at your service," Khiron laughed along with her.

"Chef Khy my ass. I didn't tell you back then, but that shit was nasty as hell! I just didn't want to bruise your precious ego."

Khiron and Mocha exited the limo once the driver held the door open for them, still laughing. Khiron held Mocha's hands all the way over to the tree. The park was full of trees and the grass was green as ever. For it to have been such a nice day Mocha was confused as to why the park was empty. She opened her mouth to ask, but Khiron was already answering.

"Money talks, Mo. You know this. I paid the city to shut this place down just for me and you," he said, opening the basket of food.

"Oh," was all Mocha could say from where she sat with her legs bent to the side. "Umm . . . what did you bring? And please don't tell me you cooked it!"

"You see, I knew you was lying way back then, 'cause a nigga like me don't cook for shit," Khiron smiled deeply. "But that's another reason why I liked you, you weren't like the other girls. You ain't just tell me what I wanted to hear, you ate that nasty ass shit too!"

Khiron pulled from the basket two cold cut sandwiches and two bags of chips. He handed her the barbecue ones, knowing they were her favorite.

"Mmm, boy you got us a gourmet meal!" Mocha joked, and Khiron gave her the side eye for her sarcasm.

The two of them ate and laughed, talking about the old times. She almost forgot the world around them. She almost forgot what was to happen that night, and she almost forgot that she hated him. But at that moment he wasn't being the man she hated, he was being the man that she loved. She was so confused and felt so guilty for enjoying her time with him. But she didn't want it to end.

"Khiron, why are you doing this?" she asked him finally, once they were done eating their food.

Khiron sat with his right leg propped up and his right arm stretched out over it. He was silent for a few moments, staring across the empty park trying to think of what he wanted to say.

"Because I love you," Khiron answered truthfully.

Mocha laughed and shook her head at his words.

"You love me?" She scoffed. "You call this love? You kill me every day without putting a bullet in my body. Love doesn't hurt, so if you *love* me why do you cause me such pain?"

"Because I hate you," Khiron told her.

"You hate me for a life that I had before you met me," Mocha said to him. She felt the pit of her stomach start to boil, and it was too late to try to stop it. She knew all of her thoughts and feelings of hostility were about to surface. "The first day you told me you loved me, I was a Last King. Throughout our whole relationship I was a Last King. I didn't hide *anything* from you, I just never had an open window of opportunity to tell you, '*Hey babe, by the way, I'm part of this underground cartel.*'

Being with you was the only get away I ever had, so when we were together I put business to the furthest part of my mind.

"How the fuck was I supposed to know that you and my best friend had any sort of sick connection? My bad, nigga, but at the end of the day my love for you was so pure. In the life that I lived with the drugs and killing, you were the only thing that made sense, the only thing that ever gave me hope! That's why I chose you. I chose you over my family, Khiron! How can you sit here and tell me you hate me when all I ever did was love you?"

Mocha had tears streaming from her eyes, but she wasn't done. Her words were now mixed with sobs, and her eyes expelled the hurt that she had kept bottled in for so long.

"How could you put me in that small ass house by myself? How could you demean me and disrespect me? *Beat* me and take my love forcefully? I *loved* you Khiron, with all my heart. I never betrayed you, not once. It was you who betrayed me."

He tried to fight it, but it was no use. Her words touched him in a place that he hadn't had feeling for a long time. He felt remorse, and no matter how much he wanted to be stubborn and say fuck what she was talking about, he knew she was right. He had been so blinded by anger that he never really took the time to look at the bigger picture. Mocha had been down for him since day one. She turned in her loyalty card for him. He killed her only family, and in turn he shunned her.

"Fuck," he said out loud and tried to reach for her. "Mocha, I'm—"

"It's too late for an apology, Khiron," Mocha said, leaning back. "You've already taken everything from me."

She didn't mention the fact that Sadie was still alive. She didn't feel the need to. As quickly as the feelings of love came, they left. Khiron was nothing but a crazy-ass nigga. The man before her was pathetic and he deserved everything he had coming to him. Maybe if he would have turned back into the asshole she was accustomed to she would have still respected him. But the fact that he showed remorse let her know that he was a nigga that didn't know how to stand by his decisions.

This nigga is the reason I been ho'ing, and he wanna say sorry, Mocha scoffed in her head. *Get the fuck outta here!*

"I'm ready to go, I have to start getting ready for tonight so I can be your arm candy, as usual."

Without another word to him, she stood up and started to make her way to where the limo was parked. Khiron shook his head and followed suit, leaving the scene of the picnic behind them. He had made one mistake, and that was showing her weakness.

Chapter 18

Tyreek sat in his car feeling like he didn't know himself anymore. He looked at the digital clock and saw that he only had a few hours to meet up with Khiron. He wasn't in his right state of mind and it felt like his car was driving itself. Somehow, he wound up outside of Mocha's house. He wanted to talk to her, needed to, but yet had nothing to say. He parked his car in her driveway and stepped out to walk slowly to her front door. He knocked softly on the door, and a part of him hoped that she didn't hear it, but she did. When she opened the door he saw that she was already fully dressed in a red Prada, sleeveless bodycon dress with a diamond choker around her neck. Her hair was pulled up in a bun at the top of her head and the make-up on her face was flawless.

"Hey, 'Reek," she said, genuinely surprised at his presence. "You're my driver?" she asked.

"Nah, I just came to talk to you," he said. "Can I come in?"

"Of course."

She let him in the house and led him to the living room. He sat down on the couch and she sat on the arm of the love seat across from him, waiting for him to say whatever was wearing on his mind. They both were holding secrets, so there were a few elephants in the room. Mocha wanted to warn him of the blood bath that lay ahead for the night, and Tyreek wanted to relinquish his guilt.

"Nervous?" Tyreek broke the silence, looking into Mocha's eyes.

"Never," Mocha lied through her teeth but kept her voice even and smooth. "This won't be the first time I have had to assume this position. What's up, though? You said you wanted to talk."

Tyreek tried to decide whether or not he wanted to tell her. He rubbed his hands together and thought back to the night that he was late getting Khiron from the airport.

The rain was falling hard on Tyreek's windshield and he could barely see. He looked at his watch and saw that he was making good time to get Khiron from the airport; he knew that nigga hated waiting.

"Damn," he said when he caught a red light.

Tapping his leg impatiently, he played with the idea of just running the light, but it would be just his luck that he would get pulled over. He didn't want to give any officer probable cause to search his vehicle, especially knowing he had a couple of concealed weapons inside of it. After a few minutes the light finally turned green again, but Tyreek was forced to stay stopped. His car was suddenly surrounded by four big black trucks. Before he could react, a small army of men hopped out of the vehicles, all with their guns drawn. He thought for sure he finally met his maker, and cursed himself for not getting bullet proof exterior for his car. To his shock, not one man fired, giving him the opportunity to get a good look at them.

"Italians," he said to himself, setting his gun on his lap with a finger around the trigger.

An older Italian man stepped forward with one of his men holding an umbrella over his head to guard him from the rain.

"Come," the man said loudly, waving his hand toward himself. "Let us talk business; I'm sure you're a man who values his life . . . and your mother's."

"Man, fuck you!" Tyreek shouted.

He ignored the idle threat, already knowing that they couldn't know where his mother was located. Barely anyone even knew his mother was still alive. He never spoke of his family to anyone; not even Khiron.

"Roll your window down so that you can hear this," the Italian man said, holding his phone up and putting it on speaker.

Tyreek eyed the phone reluctantly, but hearing the screams coming from it he did as he was told. His jaw clenched instantly and his heart beat quickened when he recognized the voice on the phone.

"No! What do you want? I don't have any money—" the voice was silenced with a smacking sound.

"Ma!" Tyreek yelled. "If you hurt her I'll kill all you mothafuckas!"

"You sure about that?" the Italian man asked. "It is in your mother's best interest that you cooperate with us. My guys tend to get a little carried away. Put that gun in the passenger's seat and get out of the car."

Tyreek breathed heavily, but knew he had no choice but to do what he was told. He threw the door open with a powerful force and walked toward the armed men.

"What do you want?" he asked when they were patting him down. The rain was drenching his clothes and he had to blink repeatedly to focus on the man who stood before him. He was happy he always kept an extra pair of clothes in his trunk. "What the fuck do you want?"

The older man smirked under the umbrella and opened his palms at his sides.

"That is simple. I want the location of the meeting with Khiron and Don Rivera."

"Fuck you," Tyreek said, not giving in so easily. His loyalty ran deep.

"Say good-bye to your mother, then," the Italian man said and started to dial a number on his phone.

"Wait!" Tyreek yelled and tried to reach for the phone. He was snatched back before one step could be taken. He jerked away from the arms and turned his head slowly around, eyeing each automatic weapon being pointed his way. These cats were playing no games, and he new that. He sighed big, knowing the decision he was about to make would be one he would regret, but what other choice did he have? "How do I know that you'll let her live once I tell you? How do I know that you won't just put two in my shit and leave her stinking somewhere?"

"You have my word," the Italian man said. "I will also give you two hundred thousand dollars for your services, but we will keep your mother as collateral until the deed is done."

Tyreek took a deep breath with his fists balled, knowing he was about to sell his brother out and sign his death wish.

Tyreek looked at Mocha and knew then that he had made a mistake by coming there. He couldn't tell her what he had done. He couldn't tell anybody. Still, when he left town that night, he didn't want to be leaving alone. He of course planned to bring his mother with him as long as the Italians held their end of the bargain, but that wasn't the woman's touch he was looking for. He stared at Mocha, who looked back questionably into his eyes. He finally understood her. The two of them weren't too different from each other. Both had sold loyalty for love. Instead of telling her what he originally had planned to, he shocked them both by going over to her and forcing her to her feet.

"Tyreek, what are you doing?" Mocha breathed. She felt one of Tyreek's hands slide onto her lower back and the other found a home on the back of her neck. "Ty—"

He didn't allow her to finish her sentence because by then his lips were already on hers. He knew it might be the last day he was able to see her, and he had always wanted to know what it would feel like to have her lips against his. Mocha kissed him passionately back and let her fragile hands grip the front of his denim shirt. There had always been a sexual tension between them, but it wasn't until then that she knew how powerful it was. She wanted him to have all of her, and she wished that she could just stay in his arms forever.

"If we would have met in another lifetime," Tyreek said to her when they broke apart, "you know you would have been mine, right?"

Mocha smiled at his words, stroking his handsome face with her hand.

"Too bad this isn't another lifetime, huh?" Mocha knew she would miss Tyreek. He had been so good to her, but that time she would choose loyalty over dick. She owed Sadie that much.

"Listen, Mo," Tyreek changed his mind again in a split second after seeing the sorrow in her eyes. "I need to tell you something important. Some shit is going to happen tonight. The Italians know about this whole meeting. It's going to be a battlefield."

Mocha gasped, and Tyreek thought she was surprised at the news he had just told her, but really she was surprised that he knew.

"Does Khiron know?" Mocha asked, scared of the answer.

"No," Tyreek said, and Mocha felt relief wash over her. "But soon he will. I don't plan on staying here until tomorrow, Mocha. I'm done with this shit. This life gets played out too soon. I don't like the fact that the people I care about most get hurt because of the lifestyle I live."

"That's what you came here to tell me?" Mocha asked.

"Yes. . . ." Tyreek said. "And to ask you to come with me. Life won't be the same, the money will be shorter. But—"

"Yes," Mocha blurted out without even thinking about it. Anything was better than the way she was living currently. "I have some money saved up. It's a little over eighty thousand dollars."

She didn't mention that it was her ho money; he might not want her to come with him anymore if he knew what she did to get that money. But little did she know, he wouldn't have cared either way. He was just glad that she had said yes.

"Okay," he was smiling from ear to ear. "You not gon' have to worry about shit, 'cause I got you!"

"Let's leave tonight!" Mocha said, not wanting to wait.

Tyreek thought about it, and when he couldn't come up with a reason why he shouldn't, he nodded his head.

"Meet me here at midnight," he said.

"If we're still alive," Mocha joked.

"We will be," Tyreek said. "We have a heads up. Which means we can duck out before the bullets get to flying. But I'm gonna go, I have to meet Khiron and your driver will be here soon. Be easy."

He kissed her on her forehead and then her lips one more time before making his exit. Little did he know, he had left her with a whole new sense of happiness.

Don Rivera stood in his room inside the penthouse suite he was inhabiting in Downtown Detroit. He was staring at a picture he had removed from his wallet. On his face there was a small smile as he looked down at the family that was ripped from him. The last time he had been to the states was a year ago. After twenty plus years, he had finally decided that it was time to make it right with the woman who had his heart. He had his share of young women, but none of them compared to his equal.

The woman who was able to match him stride for stride and fire for fire. She was the only one ever able to test his authority, because with her he had none. It tore him apart inside knowing that he would never know what it would be like to be with her again, but had been given the opportunity to make everything right. He wasn't going to mess up this time. Don heard water being ran and knew that his grandson was almost finished getting ready. Don placed the photo back in his wallet and exited the room.

Chapter 19

Showtime, Mocha thought.

Mocha walked side-by-side with Khiron in her red dress and four inch heels. Everything was a blur as she put one white pump in front of the other. The sunglasses she wore shielded her from the curious gazes of people watching the large group of people walking through the hotel lobby. Mocha, Khiron, and Tyreek walked ahead of fifteen men all wearing black suits and holding brief cases. Little did the onlookers know, but all it would take was a small flick of their wrists for those briefcases to turn into automatic weapons. When they reached the elevator, the three of them got on the first one, along with three of Khiron's goons. The others waited for the second elevator so they could follow closely behind. Everything seemed to go in slow motion. Mocha swallowed the spit forming in her mouth and she fought the urge to vomit.

"You know the drill," Khiron's voice was distant, but Mocha knew he was talking to her. "Your role is simply to sit there and look pretty. You are not to speak unless spoken to, understood?"

Mocha felt her head nod in agreement. She glanced over at Tyreek's face and saw that it was expressionless, which meant it mirrored hers. Whatever happened both of their fates were sealed. When the elevator doors opened, the goons exited first and motioned for the three of them to exit too. They'd reached as far as the elevator would take them, and walked up two flights of stairs the rest of the way to the hotel's roof top. Mocha blocked out the sounds of everything else, all she could hear was her own breath. Looking behind her, she saw that the rest of Khiron's men had caught up to them and were honing in on them. The ones who walked in front of her opened the thick, heavy door before them, and the rays of the bright sunlight that hit their faces were blinding.

The top of the building was very busy. There was a restaurant up there, and several groups of people sitting comfortably at tables under umbrellas laughing. There were people dancing and kids running around chasing after each other. The breeze was soothing, but didn't really relieve the heat from the blazing sun.

"Right there," Tyreek said, nodding toward one corner of the roof top.

Sure enough, at a table far away from all the commotion, was an older Dominican man sitting and waiting patiently. Around him stood his shooters, but Mocha was sure there were a lot more of them lurking around somewhere. Their group made their way over to him, and once there, he stood up so that he could shake Khiron's hand. His sharp brown eyes were tantalizing, and although older, he was very handsome. She held her hand out when he turned to her and he kissed it respectfully.

"Very beautiful," he said with a thick accent.

Don wanted to make the meeting short and sweet. He waited for them to sit before he smiled at them, sending uneasy chills up Mocha's spine.

"Good evening," Don said to them, giving them all eye contact, but his eyes lingered on Mocha. "Would you like a drink?"

Khiron declined.

"No, thank you," he said. "I like to have a sober mind when discussing business."

"What about the lady?"

"She can do without as well."

Don sipped his wine and looked at Khiron over the rim of his cup.

"Very respectable!" Don said, but Mocha couldn't tell if he was being serious or not. "Let us talk business then, shall we?"

Khiron nodded. This was the conversation he had been waiting on.

"You have moved quite a bit of product," Don started. "I like how you work. You are hungry but not starving. Your cartel fairs well, but it is time to put you in the seat of a king. I will front you one hundred kilos and you will only need to pay me half of that back. Use that to expand, and in the business aspect of things, the money will be doubled back to me."

Khiron didn't even think twice before accepting the proposal, and Mocha silently shook her head. A real boss knew you were never supposed to accept anything fronted, nor were you supposed to accept the first offer. A real boss would have known that there was always an underlying clause. In a way that Khiron clearly did not understand, Don had just called him incompetent. No matter how much weight Khiron moved and how much he profited, he would forever be in debt to the Dominicans. Even if Don said he wasn't. He would never be able to be a connect if his connect owned him. Accepting a front meant he had accepted the fact of being inadequate and being a flunky nigga.

He went on to tell Khiron where he would pick up the product and who he would be meeting with. Mocha saw Don slip Khiron a piece of paper and was surprised at how fast the meeting had gone, and that nothing had happened. She knew there was a tracking device in her arm, but maybe Sadie decided against retaliating against Khiron at that moment. Don stood up to make his exit, and just as Khiron was about to shake his hand again Khiron felt something fly by his cheek and saw half of one of Don's shooter's face get blown off. His blood splattered on those standing around him and his body dropped. After that it was like a ricochet effect, more bullets started flying and making their home in whoever was in their path. Everyone reacted at once. Panic erupted all around, and the whole rooftop broke out in a frenzy of blood curdling screams.

"Get down!" Mocha heard Tyreek's voice as he pushed her forcefully under the table and pulled out his gun.

Don's men surrounded him as they looked around desperately to find the source of the bullets. Tyreek reached down and grabbed Mocha by the arm.

"Get out of here, get off the rooftop!" he screamed at her.

Khiron's gun was drawn as he took cover. He looked around and all he saw were people running around, crazed and bumping into each other trying to reach the exit. There were no gaps for him to see through.

Who the fuck is shooting?

Just as the thought left his mind, there was an even louder scream by the exit door. The crowd of people backed up, and as soon as the path was cleared all Khiron heard were barks of a powerful fire arm.

Legacy gave no leeway as he fired off on the Dominicans and Khiron. He knew that once they saw their targets they would have no hold back with their clips. He wanted to drop as many of them as he could before they did so to him. Behind him, Lace and Looney made their grand entrance on the roof toting AR 22s. They were dressed in all black, not caring about the heat from the sun or what civilians they hit; if they valued their lives they would duck. The Dominicans were shouting something in a language that they didn't understand, but they began to fire back relentlessly. Legacy ran fast, ducking and dodging their fire, and hid behind a table to reload his gun. The rooftop was already a bloodbath, and he heard the loud clicking of the automatic weapons adding to it. Their snipers were clipping all of Don's shooters, and it seemed to them that they were winning. Legacy saw Khiron cowering under a table and couldn't help but aim his gun at him. Khiron must have felt like a sitting duck, because he jumped out of the way just as the bullet Legacy sent almost ended his life. Khiron busted back out of instinct and the two of them commenced to waging their own gun battle. Legacy felt heat on his arm when one of Khiron's bullets grazed it, but that did not stop him from reloading and going in for more.

"They're coming!" Legacy heard Devynn's voice come from the walkie talkie on his hip.

Looney was covering for Lace against the Dominican shooters as she ran through ducking and dodging their rapid fire to get to where Mocha was still perched. But before she could reach her, the door to the rooftop opened again, and an army of nonstop Dominican men ran atop of the roof.

"Fuck!" Lace said as she dove to take cover, just as life threatening bullets were sent her way.

She used the body of a dead teenage girl to shield her underneath a table. Looney was right behind her.

"It's too many of these muhfuckas, man!" Looney yelled over the pounding of the bullets. "Where the fuck is Tyler?"

Whoever's idea it was to put concrete tables on the roof was greatly appreciated, because they came in handy. To their luck, they didn't have to wait for very long for their Calvary to arrive. Lace felt her hair blow violently with a big gust of wind, and she heard loud noise of propellers and she smiled big when she saw the chopper.

"Right there," she answered when she saw the door to the helicopter open and Tyler standing behind it.

The Italian in the helicopter with him threw down a rope ladder as it hovered a little ways away from the building.

"We have to jump," Legacy yelled, still firing his weapon at the advancing enemy until it clicked.

"One . . . two . . . Go!" Lace yelled.

Once the three of them stood up, their snipers clipped any Dominican trying to blow their heads off. They ran to the edge of the rooftop without looking back, stepped up on the ledge and jumped. The fact that they were thirty stories up didn't dawn on them until they were hanging from the rope dangling in the open air.

"Hold on!" Legacy yelled down to Looney, who was at the end of the ladder.

Khiron ran to the edge of the rooftop with the Dominicans and looked down at the unknown attackers getting away.

"Ahh!" he yelled and pointed his gun directly at Looney and emptied his clip.

Looney didn't even know what hit him. When the bullets entered his body his eyes were looking up. Tyler saw the whole thing, but couldn't do anything to save his friend.

"No!" he yelled and tried to reach down, but it was too late. His old friend's hands loosened their grip on the rope.

"Looney!" Lace screamed, and Legacy held her tightly to him as the helicopter made its get away. She shut her eyes, not wanting to see Looney's body fall thirty stories to the ground.

"Fuck!" Legacy shouted. "Fuck! Get us out of here Tyler!"

The Italian pilot navigated through the rooftops until it reached its destination. The building was a ways away from the hotel, but he lowered them down a safe distance to let go of the rope with a rough landing. Tyler climbed down the rope and jumped, landing just barely on his feet. The helicopter made its exit, and Tyler saw Ghost and Smoke running toward them with sniper rifles still in their hands.

"Where's Loon?" Ghost asked, but seeing Tyler's face he already knew. "Damn, man."

Smoke came and patted Tyler's back one time.

"Sorry 'bout ya man, bro," Smoke said sincerely. "But come on, we gotta go."

Tyler knew that business had to continue. It was time to meet with Sadie to finish the deed.

"All right. Let's go."

Chapter 20

I sat in my Hummer, waiting patiently for my team to come back. Outside my vehicle I heard several ear splitting screams just before I heard a loud thud and crash. I hurriedly jumped out of the car and ran to where a crowd was circling around a parked SUV. What I saw made my stomach turn.

"No," I whispered as tears welled up in my eyes.

Looney's body had fallen on top of somebody's parked vehicle, and seeing his body all distorted with his bones poking out of his skin made me weak to my knees. My chest tightened and I tried to get oxygen to my lungs. His eyes were open, and as bad as I wanted to go close them out of respect, I knew with the advancing law enforcement I couldn't. Instead, I walked away and made my way back to my vehicle breathing heavily. I prayed that the others got away safely, because I couldn't get the image that I had just seen out of my head. I couldn't help but feel like I had Looney's blood on my hands. From my rearview I saw the entire hotel being evacuated and I saw Mocha exit with a darkskinned man.

I'll handle that later, I thought to myself.

I knew Don wouldn't be exiting through the front doors, but I knew Khiron would be. I assumed that Mocha would have been with him, but seeing her get inside of a different vehicle I knew I wouldn't be able to track him that way. Instead, I watched and waited patiently for him to make his exit out the front door. In the crowd of people I was finally able to spot him, he exited with precaution and made sure he had goons on every side of him. And even with them there he still looked all around, studying his surroundings.

"You shook, my nigga?" I said aloud and started my car.

I waited for his limo to pull off and started to follow it, forgetting I was supposed to be waiting for the others. I couldn't let my window of opportunity slip away though, it was now or never. I made sure that there was always a car or two between us while I tailed him, but I also made sure that I never lost sight of the limo. I followed him for about thirty minutes until I saw his limo pull into the parking lot of a nicely hidden abandoned warehouse. If I wouldn't have followed them I would have never known it was there. I kept driving so as to not draw attention to myself, but prepared to double back around. My phone started to vibrate in the cup holder and I answered as quickly as I could.

"Hello?" I asked.

"They got Loon, ma," Tyler's sad voice came through the receiver.

"I know," I said sadly. "I'm sorry, Ty. The police are all over his body. The hotel is being searched as we speak. Did everybody else make it out safe?"

"Yeah, we all good," Tyler said, and I sighed my relief. "Where are you at?"

"I'm following Khiron right now," I told him and gave him my location.

"All right, I think I know where y'all are at," Tyler said. "Crazy . . . that's where he's picking up at?"

"I'm not sure; I just know this is where this nigga is now."

"A'ight, ma, wait for us, we forty minutes away. We had to double back and swoop Dev and A."

I told him okay, although I knew I was lying. My trigger finger was itching, and the fact that my cousin's murderer was so close is what drove me to park my Hummer a few feet away, hidden under a low hanging tree. I made my way to the warehouse, strapped with three guns and two grenades. I was ready. I screwed the silencer on my pistol right before I got to the entrance of the building, and double checked my surroundings before I quietly opened the heavy door to the larger building. It was dim inside the building, and it smelled like sawdust. I held my pistol in front of me as a precaution, ready to bust on anybody who jumped. I passed several different machines that looked like they hadn't been used in years. Letting my gut instinct guide my feet I put the hood to my all black hoodie over my head. I quickly maneuvered my way through the building until I came across an old elevator. Stepping inside and shutting the gate, I pressed the red down arrow and it shook at first. I was about to get off, not wanting the rope to break, but it then began to move smoothly and my worry evaporated. Once I was on the lower level I knew I had gone the right way because I heard voices; one I instantly recognized as Khiron's. They were in a room far down the hallway, and I crept slowly toward the half way opened door. He was speaking with somebody of Dominican heritage, saying words that I couldn't quite make out. I peeked through the door and saw that Khiron had five men with him, one a Dominican man.

"Don is feeling as if you set him up," she heard the voice say. "He is not very happy."

"You have my word that I had nothing to do with that. I don't even know who those people were. Nobody knew the location of the meeting. Except you, Al." Khiron said bluntly. "Who did you all inform we were going to be there?"

His question was ignored as the man continued.

"However, Don saw you kill one of them and decided to give you the benefit of the doubt," the Dominican voice continued. "Your product will be arriving shortly."

At the reference to Looney, I lost it. I opened the door and opened fire. I had never shot my gun so quickly, but I was fueled by pure rage. In a matter of six seconds I fired six deadly shots. The Dominican connect fell back with a neat hole in the middle of his forehead as Khiron whipped around and saw me just before I sent a bullet into his shoulder blade.

"Ahh!" he said, falling back and dropping his own weapon. "Who are you?"

He was panting and in the dimmed light he couldn't make out my face. He gripped his wounded shoulder and staggered where he stood.

"Who am I?" I asked, removing my hood. "Your worst nightmare"

I wished I could have stood there forever, drinking in his look of shock mixed with confusion that turned into pure rage.

"H-how?" he asked. "I killed you!"

"Umm," I said pointing my gun at him. "Clearly you didn't. You should have, though."

I let out a crazed laugh.

"I don't know what's funnier. The fact that you thought you would get away with it, or the look on your face right now since you know you're about to die. What do you think?"

"How? I watched you die."

I lifted up my shirt and exposed my chest to him so he could get a good look at the scar from the bullet there.

"My heart is on the opposite side, bitch!" I let my shirt down, and when I saw him make another grab for his gun I shot my weapon at the space between the gun and his hand. "Ah, ah, ahhh," I waved my finger at him and took a few steps so that I could kick the gun further away from him. "Did you like the show my niggas put on for you on the rooftop? Shit was real classy, huh?"

"Yea . . . as classy as that nigga falling thirty feet, huh?" he laughed and then grimaced at the pain from his shoulder.

I sucked my teeth.

"The disrespect," I shook my head at him.

"Bitch, just shoot me," Khiron said. Sweat had started to fall from his curly head inside the non-air conditioned building, and I saw his eyes flicker quickly behind me. "That's what you came here for, right? To kill me? To get your revenge for me *killing* Ray? Well, do it then! You 'bout it, right?"

It was my turn to laugh. He was trying to goad me, and I must admit it was working.

"Okay," I said, applying pressure to the trigger of my gun. Unfortunately for me, somebody had other plans. I felt something come crashing down on my head before I got the satisfaction that I so craved. "Oomph!"

I fell to the ground with a loud thud, and just before everything went black, I heard a chuckle.

Chapter 21

My ears focused on the sound of dripping water in the distance when I finally started to come to. I kept falling in and out of consciousness, but when I focused on the sound of the water I was able to stay awake. Slowly but surely, my memories began to come back to me, but with the memories came the physical pain. My whole body ached and I didn't know if being awake was a good thing after all.

"Mmmm," I groaned.

My vision was blurred, but that didn't matter, I couldn't see anything. I tried to move my body but it wouldn't budge. It was clear at that point that I was tied to a chair in a pitch-black room. I heard footsteps walking toward me.

"Wake up, bitch," I heard a voice say.

I didn't have time to respond before I felt hot water get thrown on me. At least now I knew why I heard the sound of water dripping.

"Ahhhh! Ahhhh!" I cried out at the searing pain.

"That should wake you up," the voice said again. "Hit the lights."

Suddenly there was light, and I had to squint for my eyes to adjust. After some seconds I was able to make out the room I was in. From the look and smell of things I was still in the warehouse. My head nodded, but I forced myself to glance up at the person who had just thrown the water on me. My heart stopped when I saw that I was once again at the hands of Khiron. That time, though, he had a room full of his soldiers to back him. His arm was in a sling, and he stood over me sneering. We had only one thing in common, our hate for each other.

Khiron stared at me and I saw the monster in his eyes. He despised me before he even met me, because he was never able to compete. He hated me because he wished he was me. I hated him because he was a snake. He was a fake while I was the real thing, and that was something he was never able to accept. When he thought I was dead he had a better chance at life as a hustler. Now that I was alive he would have to kill me for real, otherwise I was going to take everything back that he *thought* was his. I would never quit coming after him. We both knew this.

"Good looks, Brandon. You came just in the nick of time," Khiron said to somebody standing behind me. He turned back to me and leered down at me. "This time, I'm going to make sure you're dead. I want to watch the life leave your body."

"Fuck you," I spat at him.

He stepped forward and punched me in my face with his free hand. My head was knocked to the side and the chair I was tied to almost came off of its legs. I immediately felt my cheek swell and I grunted at the pain.

"What did you say, I didn't quite hear you," Khiron bent down and whispered in my ear.

"I . . . said . . . fuck you. Bitch," I panted with tears in my eyes.

He punched me in the face again and again. Khiron commenced to beating me while I was helplessly tied to the chair. I knew I was going to die in that room. Even if Tyler and the others were able to reach me, it would be too late. They would probably die, too. There were just too many enemies there. I had failed. It wasn't supposed to be like this. I was supposed to come out on top this time. Instead, I had let my team down. With every punch Khiron laid on my weak body I felt more of my life being taken away from me. I spit up blood all over myself since I couldn't bend and spit it on the floor. Although he could only use one hand to punch me he was still doing me in pretty good.

"You thought you were going to win bitch? Against me?" Khiron stood back, laughing, and wiped the sweat from his face. He looked to where his men had thrown all of my weapons and got angry all over again. "You came in here prepared. You just knew you were going to kill me, huh? Grenades and shit, were you going to blow me up? You are *weak* and that's why I always win. This is my city now bitch, I won it when I killed Ray. And because you thought you would come in and take what's mine, I'm going to make you suffer."

Khiron held his hand out to one of his goons and they handed him a pair of pliers.

"Finger by finger."

Mocha pulled quickly to her house and was followed by Tyreek. He had been on the phone in his own car, but as soon as he pulled into her driveway he ended the call. Not being able to contain his happiness he jumped out of the car and ran to the house. Once inside the house, Mocha jumped into his arms.

"We're free!" she said into his neck.

"Are your bags packed, shawty?" Tyreek asked shutting the front door.

"Yes," Mocha told him letting him go and running to get her Louis Vuitton luggage.

"Cool," Tyreek said. "We need to hurry up and get to the airport."

"What about Khiron?" Mocha asked as they were on their way back out the door.

"He's not worried about us right now, ma," Tyreek said.

The way he said it made her feel like he was leaving something out.

"What's wrong?" Mocha asked stopping in her tracks. "Tell me, Tyreek."

Tyreek sighed.

He had just gotten off the phone with Khiron. He had told Tyreek he needed to come to the spot he was at to watch him handle some unfinished business. The unfinished business was Mocha's old best friend . . . Sadie. Khiron said that somehow she had survived his bullet wounds and had come back to retaliate. It made sense to Tyreek. It all clicked. That's why the Italians wanted the information about the meeting, for Sadie. He looked at Mocha and his selfishness guided him to give his response.

"Nothing, I'm just ready to go," Tyreek said. "I don't want him to know shit, even when we're gone."

Mocha smiled, knowing that he didn't have to worry about that. She knew Khiron would be dead soon. Sadie would handle that.

"Okay," Mocha went up to him and kissed him sensually. "Let's go."

Tyler drove like a mad man trying to get to Sadie. He knew her, and he knew she hadn't waited like he had asked her to. When he was on the phone with her he heard the hidden rage in her voice, she was just like him. He was worried something bad had happened to her. There was something about the whole situation that wasn't sitting right with him. He would have never continued business with a man after being attacked in his city. That was certainly a set up. But Don was still going to give Khiron more work. What made it even more unsettling was the location that Sadie had given him.

Only two people knew about that building, and Tyler was one of them. How did the Dominicans know it existed? And even if they did somehow know of its location, why would they choose it as the pick-up spot? Tyler shook his head trying to make sense of all of his thoughts.

"Say should have waited for us," Devynn broke the silence, knowing that Sadie had gone in solo. "She would have called us by now asking where the fuck we're at. . . ."

She let her voice trail because fear was coursing through her chest. She prayed that Sadie was okay. That was her sister; blood couldn't have made them any closer.

"She's okay," Adrianna said, but when she turned to Tyler her voice cracked, betraying her. "Drive faster!"

Adrianna had already lost Ray, she couldn't lose Sadie too. Losing Ray had broken her heart and Sadie was her only living and breathing link to him. When she looked into Sadie's eyes she saw Ray, that's how she was able to move on. She had a bad feeling that something horrible had happened to their little sister, and everybody that could help was sitting there in that truck. Devynn was right, Sadie would have called by now complaining about how they needed to hurry up. Adrianna didn't know that Sadie's judgment would be that clouded, but if the tables were turned, Adrianna knew that she would have dived in head first as well. Still, that knowledge didn't make her feel any better, especially knowing what kind of evil she was up against.

"Hold on, mama," Adrianna whispered. "We're coming for you."

Chapter 22

Khiron walked slowly toward me with a sick smile on his face. My eyes were swollen and could only open in slits. The way my head throbbed and swayed, I was certain I had internal bleeding. When he was close enough to touch me again I clenched my hand around the arm of my chair, but he pried it free.

"Don't worry, shawty," Khiron said smoothly. "This will be *very* painful. Feel free to scream."

I felt the plier clench my pointer finger tightly and I bit my lip at the growing pain, knowing my finger was about to be gone.

"Enough!" I heard a voice say loudly, and instantly the pain lessened.

Weakly, I held my head up and tried to focus on the source of the voice. What I saw was a man dressed in a two-button suit who was clearly of Dominican descent. Behind him was his own small army of Dominican soldiers, all with their weapons drawn.

"Don," Khiron started seeing the loaded guns. "No disrespect, but this bitch is the one who sent the shooters to the roof. She has to die."

Don Rivera looked toward where I sat barely conscious and I struggled to keep his eye contact. There was something very familiar about his eyes, but before I could put my finger on it. He turned back to Khiron. I sat in the chair, breathing rigidly trying to hold on to every little bit of life still within me. I knew that if I didn't get a grip on things I would pass out again. I had too much trauma to my head and needed medical attention badly. My vision was going in and out and blood kept seeping out of my mouth. I was sure that I looked like shit.

"Like I said," Don said briskly, almost angrily. "Enough. You are here to conduct business, instead you are wasting your time torturing a woman."

Don studied Khiron's anguished face.

"You hate her that much?" Don looked at Khiron and shook his head.

He walked past Khiron to where I sat in the chair and studied my bruised face. I could barely focus on him since he was so close, but I thought I saw a concerned expression make its way to his face. If I did, it exited as quickly as it came.

"I know who you are," he said to me in a low smooth voice. "Your cartel is one that even the highest of cartels envy. For that, I have to give you my respect."

"If y—if you're going to kill me," I said weakly, "I—I don't need to hear you pay me your respects."

My head nodded, but I kept trying to focus on his face.

"Why are you here?" Don asked me calmly, like I wasn't sitting before him fading in and out of consciousness.

"I," I panted, "was going to kill him before you hit me in the head like a bitch."

"I, my dear, just got here," he said, kneeling down before me. "It was not me who knocked you out. But someone of your stature should have known coming in here alone was a bad idea. Khiron had the place crawling with his men. Right, Khiron?"

He turned his head to Khiron, who was standing

"I am not going to kill you," Don said. "In fact, I am about to spare your life."

"What, nigga?" Khiron said, forgetting who he was speaking to. "You're just here to drop off my work."

"This is business," Don said to him. "She is connected to the Italians, which means she is my problem to handle. You, my friend, have your own problems to deal with."

"No," Khiron said. "We have some unfinished business to tend to."

"And I am telling you that it is finished," Don said in a tone that suggested that the conversation was done. "Cut her loose!"

I felt the ropes around my arms, legs, and torso being cut, and I fell onto the ground on my hands and knees. I threw up everything in my stomach, and when I was done there was nothing but a bloody mess on the floor. My arms shook, and right when I wasn't able to hold myself up anymore I felt my body get scooped up off of the ground. Whoever held me was muscular and strong and they cradled me like a baby. I looked up and was staring into the face of a handsome man with sleek hair. He stared back down at me and studied my face. Sadness overcame his eyes. He wasn't rough with me at all, he was surprisingly gentle and held me delicately.

"Take her to my car," Don instructed and looked at me in my current state. "I will be there shortly. I have a deal to wrap up here."

The man carried me out of the room in the abandoned warehouse, and I tried to stay conscious to see exactly where we were going. I didn't want any surprises. I had no reason to trust them, especially with the feud that was going on. The man was accompanied by one more Dominican man, and they spoke to each other quickly.

Stay with me, Sadie, I thought to myself when my eyes closed.

I forced my eyes to stay open, and suddenly the bright sunlight evaded my eyes and I felt the sticky heat on my bruised body. I saw that the door to the limo he was carrying me to was open before we reached it, but that was as much as I saw before I lost the energy to keep my eyes open. The trauma to my head was taking its toll on me, and I knew it wouldn't be long before I lost consciousness.

"She needs to get to the hospital," I heard the Dominican voice say. "She was not supposed to be here. He beat her pretty bad."

I was confused. Why would the Dominicans take me to the hospital? The hospitals nursed a person back to health. I couldn't understand why Don Rivera would want to save my life.

"He did this to her?" I heard a muffled voice say right before I passed out. "A'ight."

Everything went black.

Chapter 23

Khiron stood on one side of the room with his goons, and Don Rivera stood on the other side with his. Khiron's arm throbbed, bent in his manmade sling, and the fist that he used to punch Sadie repeatedly was sore.

Where the fuck is Tyreek? What the fuck kind of time is this nigga on? Khiron thought, knowing that his right hand should have been there by now.

"That was very unfortunate for you to do," Khiron said to him.

"My apologies," Don said with a small smile. "But, once again, you and I have bigger matters to deal with than you killing her."

"You saved her," Khiron glared at the man before him, uncertain about his next move.

Khiron knew that with Sadie surviving again had just put his own life on a count down. He knew that she would not stop coming for him until he was dead. He cursed himself for not lighting her body up with clip after clip when he left her in her grandmother's house. He should have sent a bullet through her head, instead of her chest, just like he had done her grandmother. She died instantly.

"It was in your best interest," Don told him.

"She killed your men on the rooftop," Khiron said to Don, trying to convince him that he was making a mistake by letting her survive. "She's a liability if she is allowed to still have breath."

Don just stared at Khiron and started to laugh.

"Let us continue business, shall we?" Don said. "You will have plenty of time later for all of that."

Don waved for one of two of his men to come forward, and they placed two suitcases in front of the chair that Sadie had just been cut free from. Khiron was confused. One hundred kilos couldn't fit in two suitcases. Don stared at Khiron and let the hate in his eyes show at that very moment. Khiron furrowed his brow, but before he could even inquire on what the look was for, the Dominicans opened fire on all of Khiron's goons behind him.

"Shit!" Khiron yelled, dropping to the ground, throwing his good hand up to protect himself from the bullets.

He felt blood splatter on him, and just as fast as the gunfire had started, it stopped. Breathing heavily, Khiron whipped his head behind him and saw that all his niggas lay in their own blood. He saw Brandon laying on his back, staring into the air blankly with a single neat bullet hole in his head. Khiron saw the deep red blood running toward him on the floor and took several steps away from it. They had been caught off guard, and not one of them had a gun drawn. Khiron tried to reach for his waist, but he was too slow. He felt a sharp kick on his injured arm and he instantly saw red due to the pain.

"Tie him up," he heard Don Rivera say.

Khiron felt somebody take his gun from his waist and hoist his body up into the chair.

"Yo man, what the fuck are you doing? Ahh!" Khiron yelled in pain when his arm was ripped from the sling to be tied to the arm of the chair.

He tried to struggle against the Dominicans and managed to break one arm free, but that was no use because he was just grabbed again. His efforts were futile.

Once they had him tied to the chair he fought against his restraints, but it was no use, all he was doing was moving the chair around the room.

"Man, I ain't set you up on top of the roof!" Khiron shouted.

He had never been in such a position in his life. He was sure Don was retaliating because Dominicans were killed on the rooftop. Don must have thought Khiron was a set-up nigga, and if that was the case, Khiron knew he only had a few seconds to clear up the confusion. Khiron knew what he was capable of and he was not ready to die.

"That was that bitch you just set free! You got the wrong nigga."

Don walked slowly away from his entourage toward Khiron and stopped when he was directly in front of him looking down.

"I know that was not you," Don sneered. "That mission was carried out too smoothly. It was thought out and planned to a T. It was almost flawless. That is something I am sure you are not even capable of doing. If your dead friend over there wouldn't have come at the right time, then the mission would have been completed."

"What are you doing this for then?" Khiron snarled, trying to contain his fear. "I thought we were supposed to be conducting business."

Don Rivera just stared directly into Khiron's eyes, furrowing his brow.

"You are scared of death," Don said, not ever blinking. "You take lives daily, live a lifestyle that death follows, but yet here you are strapped to this chair, afraid to die."

Khiron said nothing; he just returned the look of hatred back.

"You have already lost, but yet you have not accepted your fate," Don took a step back. "The thing that you still don't realize, however, is that you sealed your fate away a year ago."

Don saw that Khiron still was not catching his drift, so he figured he would show him. He walked over to the first suitcase and picked it up. Opening it, he pulled out the contents, placing the suitcase back on the ground.

"She was a very beautiful woman," Don said, looking at what he had in his hands. "Your mother was."

He threw each of the pictures he was holding down on the ground before Khiron, and Khiron couldn't breathe looking at the images.

"Ma," he said, his chest heaving. "Ma!"

The images vividly showed his mother laying naked, tied up to a bed on top of all white sheets that were now stained red. Her whole body was full of deep gashes and her throat was slit ear to ear. Each picture was a different angle of his mother's gruesome murder. His screamed got louder and louder.

"You don't like my art work? I call it 'Chop Shop,'" Don laughed at Khiron's attempts to break away from the chair he was bound to. "You shouldn't strain your shoulder, you do have a bullet in it, you know."

Khiron fought the tears in his eyes. His mother had died in the most painful way. The woman that had given him life was dead.

"Bitch!" Khiron yelled. "I'm going to kill you, mothafucka!"

Don laughed again.

"I don't think so," Don said, shaking his finger. "I'm a firm believer in 'what goes around, comes around.'"

Don grabbed the second suitcase and opened it up. From that one he pulled out one single photo. He held it in his hands and just stared at it.

"I was in love once," Don said, his voice quiet as he stared at the picture. The iciness in his tone was so cold that Khiron almost shivered from where he was bound.

"She was an amazing woman. I loved her with all my heart. Much like you loved your dead mother there. I made one mistake. I chose the world of drugs over my family. I was not able to keep her happy because of my infatuation with money. I thought that I would be able to buy her happiness. I was wrong.

"She tried to love me, even through her unhappiness, but eventually she couldn't take it anymore. She packed her bags and our children . . . and left me. I was too proud to chase after her. That was my biggest mistake. She raised our children here by herself, and they turned out horrible. They were rich but were raised poor because she didn't want anything to do with me. My son was killed, and my daughter is somewhere strung out probably dying too. I came back to the states a year ago to find my wife . . . nobody could replace her. I was never happy with anybody else. She was my soul mate. We came from two different worlds but were perfect for each other."

Don looked up from the photo, and if looks could kill, Khiron would have been dead right then and there. Don placed the photo on Khiron's lap.

"I found her address and I was too late. The paramedics were wheeling her body out . . . the back of her head was blown off. She was murdered and I wasn't there to protect her. But what she left me was something more valuable than my cartel itself. She gave me a second chance to make things right within my family."

Khiron took that moment to look down at the photo and his eyes became saucers on his face. His mouth opened wide and he inhaled sharply. The picture was a family portrait, and in it was an older black woman; she was beautiful for her age. But that isn't what had caused him to gasp. Standing on either side of her was a beautiful young woman and a young man who had growing dreads. They both had the same matching, sharp brown eyes.

"Get it now?" Don said. "You killed the love of my life. She didn't deserve to die, but you still took her and any chance we had away from me. The funny thing is, her life wasn't the only one you took that night."

Khiron saw the men behind Don clear out the way.

"It's time for you to taste your karma," Don smiled sinisterly at Khiron. "I'd like to introduce you to my grandson."

Everything was quiet and seemed to go in slow motion, and Khiron heard the footsteps of someone walking toward the entrance to the room before he saw him. The man who entered the room was tall and muscular, his brown skin had some light patches on it, and he no longer had dreads. Instead he had a brush cut, but his face didn't really look very different besides the light patches on it, and his lack of facial hair.

"Remember me?" the man said, smirking, raising his gun and aiming it directly at Khiron. "I told you kings don't die, nigga."

"Ray," Khiron spoke the name like he had seen a ghost, just before Ray fired his weapon.

Chapter 24

Tyler was almost to the warehouse when he felt his phone vibrate in his pocket. Fearing that it was Sadie, he quickly grabbed it from his pocket.

"Hello?" he answered, not looking at the caller ID. "Sadie?"

"Change of plans," he heard Vinny's voice come through the other end of the phone. "Sadie is okay, the Dominicans have her."

Tyler was alarmed.

"What the fuck?" Tyler yelled through the phone. "What the fuck do you mean they have her? Where the fuck is she at?"

He couldn't lose Sadie. He had already had the fear of losing someone he loved once, and now that he knew she was safe, he couldn't feel that pain again. He was pissed at Vinny for not moving on them if he knew they had Sadie.

"I have somebody following their car. I believe they are headed to the hospital. Go. Now!"

"Where will you be?" Tyler asked as he busted an illegal U-Turn on the interstate.

Cars honked and cursed him, but he didn't give a fuck. Fuck them.

"I will be there soon," Vinny said and disconnected the call.

"Aye, man!" Devynn yelled from the backseat. "What the fuck is up?"

"The Dominicans have Sadie, they're on their way to the hospital."

"They'll kill her," Adrianna said. "If she's not already dead."

"Why the hospital, though?" Lace asked.

"Just drive!" Legacy barked from the backseat. "Shut the fuck up with the questions. Niggas have already wasted enough time."

Tyler sped the whole way to the hospital. He couldn't believe what was happening. He kept having horrible daydreams of walking into the hospital and seeing Sadie's dead body sprawled on the floor with several bullet holes.

"Nah, ma," Tyler said under his breath. "Don't die on me."

Adrianna grabbed his hand as a gesture to let him know that everything would be okay. She knew what it felt like to lose the love of your life, and she didn't wish that on anybody.

"I'm going to dead each and every one of them Dominican mothafuckas if they touch a hair on my baby's head," Tyler growled. "I put that on my life."

Mocha and Tyreek made it to the airport with looks of determination on their faces. They were so close to freedom they could taste it. Tyreek helped Mocha out of the car and went to the back to grab their bags. Dressed in a floral romper and gold gladiator sandals, Mocha was making her way to the revolving doors and didn't think to look back at Tyreek to see what the holdup was.

Tyreek turned around to follow Mocha with the luggage, but when he turned around, he crashed into somebody and dropped the luggage.

"My bad," Tyreek said annoyed.

"It is okay," he heard somebody say, and the accent he heard was one he was familiar with.

Tyreek looked up into the face of a young Italian man with jet black hair.

"I have a message from Vinny," Victor said with a sharp knife in his hand.

Before Tyreek could reach for his gun, Victor had already stabbed him repeatedly four times, the last time putting the knife so far in Tyreek's stomach that blood expelled from his mouth. Victor placed his mouth close to Tyreek's ear as he staggered back to the car he had just exited.

"Vinny said *he* wouldn't kill you. He never said I couldn't."

Victor quickly opened the back door of the vehicle and laid Tyreek along the backseat before shutting the door. He put the luggage back in the trunk then pulled off, checking his surroundings. Everyone was too busy bustling around trying to make sure they were on time for their flights to even notice the murder.

Mocha had gotten a ways away, and when she realized Tyreek hadn't caught up to her yet she turned around, expecting to see him coming up behind her.

"Where this nigga at?" she asked aloud, stepping on her tippy toes to see over the big crowd of people. "That nigga got all my shit and we gon' miss our flight!"

She started to go back the way she came when she felt a hand grab her arm.

"Baby, I thought I had lost you!" she said, turning around smiling, but instantly the smile was wiped away when she saw the person who had grabbed her arm wasn't Tyreek.

She had never seen him in person but she knew who he was. Vinny eyed her for a few moments before shaking his head at her. Everything that had taken place was because of her. If only she had stayed true to the code of every hustler before her.

"Tyreek is dead, and it is time for you to come with me."

His request wasn't up for discussion, because he grabbed her arm to lead her toward the exit. She obliged without fighting it. She didn't know why she thought she was going to be able to get away without having to face her past sins.

"Where are you taking me?" she asked once they were settled inside of an empty limo.

Vinny said nothing, instead he grabbed two glasses and poured two shots. Handing one to her, he held his in the air waiting for her to clank her glass with his. She saw what he wanted her to do, and she did so reluctantly and threw back the shot of Patrón.

"Mocha," Vinny started as the limo drove. "I have been watching you. Mostly I have been watching those around you. I noticed Tyreek's growing infatuation with you. And the fact that he would even allow himself to catch any type of feelings for his best friend's girlfriend put a big question mark on his loyalty to Khiron. I knew that if I came at him he would break and give me the destination of the meeting with Don Rivera, and I also knew that if I offered him money he would try and skip town. Most cowards share the same traits, so he was very predictable. I guessed that he would come to you and ask you to come with him."

"All this to get to me?" Mocha asked. "If you had been watching me like you claimed why not just come get me from my house?"

Vinny chuckled.

"What fun is that?" He smiled at her.

They were silent the rest of the way to their destination, and when Mocha saw that they had reached the hospital she looked curiously to Vinny.

"Why are we here?" She asked him.

"Room 851," was all Vinny said, looking the other way. "Get out."

Mocha feared him having to ask again, so she did as she was told. She looked back at him, but he was already pulling away. Unsure of why she was there, she made her way to the inside of the hospital. Trying not to think about Tyreek, she walked toward the elevator, making sure to check every corner. Knowing the people she was dealing with, she didn't put anything past anybody. Niggas weren't scared to pop off on top of a hotel roof, so she for damn sure knew they weren't afraid to do it in a hospital. The majority of the patients were dying anyway. So much had happened that day she didn't know what to expect. After the whole hotel fiasco Mocha had no idea what had gone on with Sadie or if they were even still alive. Sadly, she couldn't say whether she cared or not. Mocha wanted to cry because of how close to freedom she was. The longer she stayed in Detroit the bigger the target on her head got.

Once she was inside of the vacant elevator she closed her eyes and let it take her eight stories up. She thought back to the day she sold out The Last Kings to Khiron.

"Bring that ass here," he bit his lip at her and she smiled, sashaying his way.

"Mmm, you ready for me already?" Mocha said seductively, straddling him.

"Nah, chill, ma," Khiron placed his hands on her waist, stopping her from grinding on him. He knew he wouldn't be able to stop her once she got going. "I just wanna kick somethin' to you right quick."

Mocha cocked her head at him and eyed him with her light brown eyes, curious as to what he had to say.

"Well, speak, nigga," Mocha told him. "This pussy can't wait all day."

Khiron thought quickly about his plan, knowing that everything about it was pointing against him, but putting Mocha in the know was the only way she would sing information. If it didn't work it would be nothing to just put her to sleep forever in that hotel suite.

"I know about you, ma," Khiron started, and immediately saw the look on her face go from pleasured to nervous.

"Know about me?" Mocha giggled, trying to catch herself. "I would hope you know me. You've been fuckin' with me for a while now, bae. Now come here and make me feel good."

"Nah, Mocha," Khiron pushed her hands off of him. "You know what I mean. The Last Kings ring a bell?"

Mocha's face paled and she stood to her feet.

"Were you ever going to tell me?" Khiron asked her, seriously wanting that answer.

"No," Mocha didn't even have to think before she answered, and that made Khiron even more angry than when he got wind of who she really was.

Mocha saw the anger in Khiron's face and couldn't help not giving a damn. She didn't feel that Khiron needed to know about her business dealings. It wasn't any of his business. She also didn't inform him of her affiliation in fear that he would try and use her connections for his own personal gain. She felt something in the air change between them, and she didn't like or trust it. She knew how Khiron got down. She wouldn't have kept visiting him in Atlanta if she didn't do some kind of research. His body count stretched a long way; he'd killed mercilessly to obtain his spot as Atlanta's boss, so she knew that he was nobody you wanted to go toe to toe with. Khiron just nodded his head.

"I met with Ray a few nights ago," Khiron's intentions were no longer to keep his words sweet. He wanted to cut her deep to the core. "That nigga, he's a true boss I'm not gon' hate on 'em. But every boss gets caught slippin', right?"

Mocha stopped dressing herself and stared at Khiron in only a pair of shorts and her bra. The mood had been killed for her and her mindset was changing from girlfriend Mocha to Last King Mocha. The man before her was not the man she loved. The look in his eyes held something completely different. It was the look of a hungry dog.

"The fuck are you talkin' about, Khiron? The Last Kings don't get caught slipping, least of all Ray, so quiet that noise."

Khiron stood up and walked slowly to the night stand beside his bed. From it he pulled out a machete. The same machete he used to kill D and Amann in fact, it still was stained with their dried up blood.

"I'm assumin' that's what those other two niggas thought? Right?" He smirked at Mocha and her mouth dropped.

"Y-you?" Mocha's mind reeled looking at the weapon. "You killed my bros?"

Khiron's connect was just sent to prison and he had just said he had a meeting with Ray. She remembered Adrianna mentioning something about a meeting with someone from Atlanta that he turned away. Mocha didn't really pay her any mind since Ray had a lot of business meetings. Standing there, she wished she'd paid more attention and hadn't left her gun in the car. She backed up as far as she could until her back was pressed up against the wall, and Khiron advanced on her.

"What do you want, Khiron?" she asked him. "Why did you kill them?"

"I want it all," Khiron smiled, knowing his answer answered both questions. "I'm going to kill anyone in the way of what's mine."

In Khiron's crazy way of thinking, Ray's operation was rightfully his since it was given to him by Khiron's father's killers.

"No!" Mocha cried out. "You bitch! You didn't come here to see me . . . you're trying to take the city, our city."

"Yea," Khiron shrugged. "Pretty much, and you're going to help."

"Fuck you," Mocha tried to make a dash for the door, but Khiron grabbed her forcefully by her neck.

Mocha was a fighter, but her punches did nothing to Khiron's big build. Her energy was fading along with her breath, so she stopped fighting after a few seconds. Khiron pinned her back up against the wall, but as he opened his mouth to speak his phone vibrated with a message. Knowing what it was about he glanced at it, smiled, and turned his attention back to the woman he was suffocating.

"I don't want to kill you Mocha, but I swear to God I will," Khiron's voice was like venom and Mocha's body was paralyzed.

She felt hot tears coming to her eyes as she gulped for air. She stared into the cold eyes of the man she once loved and felt nothing but hatred. She saw her life flash before her eyes when his grip around her neck tightened and then loosen.

"I know you, Mocha. You're not a hustler and you're not a killer. You kind of just fell into this profession, and I want to take you out. Your place is beside the man in charge," Khiron decided to change up his approach. "I'm so sorry, babe; I don't want to hurt you. You know I love you, ma, but this is business. A woman of your caliber shouldn't have to work, ever. Help me, ma. And I promise I got you."

Mocha's mind was reeling. Her loyalty was to the Last Kings, and a part of her wanted to spit in his face *for what he was implying she do. But another part of her had to admit that he was right. The cartel was and had always been Sadie's idea; Mocha was just her ride or die. But now faced with the presence of death she knew she wasn't ready to perish. The lavish life she lived came with a price, and with every heart her bullets pierced a piece of her soul left her body. She felt like a traitor, she had said she would go to the grave for her team. The tattoo branded on her body made that promise, but promises were meant to be broken. After the deaths of D and Amann the pain she felt was unbearable, and feeling the tears trailing down her face she knew the Last Kings would never be the same. She knew she only had seconds to make her decision.*

"Just promise me one thing," Mocha choked on her tears and closed her light brown eyes. "And I'll do whatever you want."

Khiron felt the sticky smile forming slowly on his face.

"Name it," he wiped the tears from her face like he wasn't the one causing them.

"Sadie lives," Mocha's eyes shot open and there was a fire so strong in them Khiron almost took a step back.

He studied her, knowing that if he said no he would have to kill her and find another way of getting to Ray in a day's time. But he also knew that what she was asking for was a promise that he couldn't keep. Still, he looked into her eyes and put on the most sincere face he could muster.

"You have my word, ma," the lie burned on his tongue, and he cupped her face. "I promise."

Mocha heard the ding that let her know that she had reached the floor she needed to be on and she wiped away her tears. She wished every day that she could redo that day, but it was something that God wouldn't permit.

That day Khiron had taken her out on a picnic, although it was a sweet gesture, held no real meaning. He had still tried to take everything from her, but he failed. She would never forgive him, the same way she understood why Sadie would never forgive her.

She looked at all the numbers on the room's doors, and when she found her destination she opened the door softly. To her surprise, she found it full of people. There were many faces she didn't know, but she did recognize Devynn, Adrianna, and Tyler. When they saw her, the look of distaste was apparent on their faces.

"What's going on?" she asked the room of people, but nobody said anything, they just ignored her. "I know you mothafuckas hear me!"

"We just got here too, nigga," Devynn snapped, glaring at Mocha, but she ignored her and looked directly to the hospital bed.

Laying there with her eyes wide open was Sadie. Sadie looked like shit. It looked like somebody had literally beaten her to a bloody pulp. They stared at each other but before either could speak. Mocha rushed over to her former best friend's side.

"Say," Mocha said with her lip quivering. "What happened? Did the Dominicans do this to you?"

Sadie looked around her at everybody in the room and shook her head.

"No," she said. "The Dominicans didn't do this to me, Khiron did. I was about to kill him, but I ended up getting got and *ahh* . . . the Dominicans. Well, the Dominicans saved me."

The room became loud several confused outbursts.

"Why would they do that?"

"Are you sure, Sadie? You got hit in your head a lot of times."

"They *saved* you? Was Don Rivera there?"

"What about the feud?"

"There was no real feud," They heard a voice boom from over the noise. "And yes, I was there."

Everybody turned around to see an older Dominican man that they all recognized as Don Rivera himself. He saw all the confused stares and smiled, bowing his head quickly as an apology for the miscommunication. Everyone was silent and everybody, even Legacy, stepped out of his way as he made his way to Sadie's bed. He stared at her fondly, like she reminded him of somebody, and then he smiled.

"It is true that I was angered by the actions of the Italians, but Vinny is very silly to think that I would start a war because of that. As a business man I understand that his decision was strictly a business one. But, however, I needed him to believe that there was a feud. And we needed you to believe so as well, Sadie. All of this was to get a common enemy: Khiron."

"We?" Sadie asked, confused.

"Yes, we," Don said.

Don turned to Tyler and handed him a slip of paper.

"Here is your plane ticket; go get your sister," Don told him. "Your flight leaves in a few hours. You need to get going now. The rest of you need to clear this room. Now."

He dismissed Tyler, and the rest of them by turning his back on them.

"How can I trust you?" Tyler asked skeptically.

"If I wanted to kill you, I would, right here and now. I wouldn't go out of my way to."

Tyler stared at Don, whose back was still to him. Tyler noticed how he looked at Sadie. He stared at her as if he loved her.

"Leave," Tyler told the rest of them. "Go back to the house. Except you, Mocha."

There were some protests, but they knew better than to test Tyler's authority. Legacy gave Tyler a look and Tyler just nodded. When they were all gone Tyler looked to Don. Ever since Don had given Khiron the address of the warehouse to meet him something hadn't been sitting right with him. There was something about Don that Tyler just couldn't put his finger on.

"Who are you?" Sadie asked him, looking deep into his eyes. "Why did you save me?"

"Rae would never forgive me if I let anything happen to you. She would turn over in her grave," he said simply, walking toward her bed and grabbing her hand. "I wouldn't be able to forgive myself."

"Y-you knew my grandmother?" Sadie breathed.

Don smiled deeply.

"Yes, very well, actually," Don squeezed her hand slightly. "She was my wife. I loved her and your mother deeply."

Mocha gasped, and Tyler stood there looking dumbfounded.

"My grandmother was your wife? You knew my mother? But ho—no. . . ." Sadie finally understood.

"Your mother is my daughter, Sadie. And that makes you my granddaughter. I came back to avenge Rae's death, and in turn I found two of the last of my direct bloodline."

"You found my mother?" Sadie asked. "How is she?"

Don shook his head.

"I didn't find your mother," he said.

"Then who did you—"

They all heard the door open and heard a voice so familiar they all thought that someone was playing a cruel joke on them.

"What's up, shorty?"

Chapter 25

I felt tears rush to my eyes as I stared at the most beautiful face in the world. No he didn't look the same—and no, his face wasn't unblemished—but standing there he looked more perfect than ever.

"Ray," I barely whispered. "Ray . . . Is that really you?"

I forgot about my bruises and aches in my body as I struggled to sit up in my bed. I wanted more than ever to run to him and cling to him, but my current state wouldn't allow that. Instead he walked over to me and wrapped his arms around me as tightly as he could without hurting me. Don stood to the side, smiling as he watched the reunion of The Last Kings, minus two. I cried hard into his neck and thanked God in my head.

"I knew it, nigga!" Tyler gave a triumphant laugh. "Niggas can't kill a real king! I knew some shit was up when Don wanted to meet at the warehouse you were in the process of creating."

Mocha just stood there, her feet were frozen to the ground. She stared at Ray's brush cut and the light blotches on his skin and I saw the look of remorse spread across her face. She could barely keep her balance.

"How?" she whispered. "I saw you die."

"You thought you saw me die," Ray said, looking at Mocha indifferently. "After the acid hit me it ate away at some of my flesh, but it didn't penetrate my organs. Just because I was still and not breathing didn't mean I was dead. Khiron left the building without checking my pulse, and Don Rivera found me when the cleaning team was on its way to get me. The bone in my arm was almost completely eaten away," Ray looked at his arms, but you could barely tell anything was wrong with them. "I had to go through over half a year of cosmetic surgery and undergo several other bodily surgeries just to look like this again. The hair on my head might grow back eventually, but if not it's cool. I'm starting to grow fond of the no hair look. Don shipped me away to Azua once I was able to be moved, and I have lived there ever since."

"What about the video?" I asked. "You said you were dead."

"I did make that, just in case I died," Ray smiled at me.

I studied my cousin's face and saw that although he was scarred for forever and his life would never be the same, he still was very handsome.

"Tyler," Ray's voice changed from sweet to business in a matter of seconds. "Get everybody out of here, Sadie needs to rest. Have the doctor bring in some pain medication for her; she will need all the strength she can muster tomorrow. Mocha, you can stay."

"A'ight, man," Tyler slapped hands with his right hand man, still not believing he was alive and upset that there was no time to celebrate it. "I'll catch y'all tomorrow evening."

When everybody left except for Ray and Mocha, Don tried to convince me to go to sleep, but I couldn't. Before, I would go to sleep just so I could see Ray in my dreams, but at that moment I felt I didn't need to. My dreams had come true. Don sat in a chair staring curiously at me, and Ray commenced to talking to me; answering all of my questions. Mocha sat in a chair looking uncomfortable, but her eyes never left my hospital bed. Finally, the nurse came in and gave me something for my pain and to help me sleep. I tried to fight off the drowsy feeling overcoming my body in fear that once I closed my eyes Ray would be gone again when I woke up, but it was no use. I was out in less than five minutes.

The next day I woke and was pleased to see the same faces I went to sleep to still there, just in different clothes. My body was still very sore, but whatever the doctor prescribed me was working wonders. I knew my face was still puffy and I was positive my eye was black, but the aching had become dormant. My eyes first fell on Don Rivera's.

"You're still here?" I asked.

"Of course," was all he said. It was all he had to say, and I smiled.

I looked at the clock and saw that it was almost three o'clock in the afternoon.

"I had the doctor prescribe you some of their strongest pain killers," I heard Ray's voice say. "We have some unfinished business to handle; I needed you to be able to move. Can you walk?"

Even if I couldn't, I knew I was going to force myself. I didn't want to stay in that hospital bed longer than I had to. The aching was mostly in my head and my face, so I figured I would be okay. After standing to my feet, Mocha handed me a handful of clothes.

"Thank you, Mo," I said.

I quickly got dressed and allowed Don Rivera to push me in a wheel chair out of the hospital to his limousine, not knowing where we were going. In the limousine I sat so close to Ray you would have thought I was a tampon up his ass, while Mocha kept her distance, as she should.

"Where did you leave him?" Don asked Ray.

"Gun range," Ray answered simply.

Don smiled at Ray and nodded his head in approval. I didn't understand exactly what they meant, and for once instead of asking I just sat, waiting to find out. I felt indifferent. I knew that day was going to be a big day, but until that moment I didn't know how big.

"I heard they got Loon," Ray broke the silence.

"Yeah," I said sadly. "That muhfucka was trained to go."

"Yeah," Ray said nodding his head. "That nigga was thorough. Wish it didn't have to be him; any of you for that matter."

We rode the rest of the way making small talk, and Don looked at us very intrigued.

"You both remind me so much of her. Thank you," he said and smiled.

"No," I said to him earnestly. "Thank you. If it weren't for you my cousin really would be dead. How did you know to go to Amore that night?"

"Vinny and I did great business together back then. He would often brag about the food and drinks there, so I decided to go. In a way, I knew I was supposed to be there. I was confused as to why the restaurant was empty, yet the doors were not locked. I saw Khiron give the order to kill Ray, but before that I heard him confess to the murder of your grandmother, and at the time you."

I nodded my head, thankful for the fact that his heart had brought him back to Grandma Rae even though it didn't work in his favor with her. I looked at Mocha with hate in my eyes, and she looked back at me with hope in hers.

"I'm surprised you haven't skipped town yet," I told her.

"What good would that do?" Mocha shot back. "You would just track me down."

She motioned to her shoulder and I remembered the tracking device Adrianna put there. Looking at me, I knew she wanted to say something, but as my former best friend I knew exactly what she was thinking. She wanted me to forgive her, especially since Ray was alive after all, and to continue being best friends like nothing had ever happened. She wanted me to show her real love, break bread with her once again, and to be my ride or die again.

"We're here," Ray said, interrupting our wordless conversation.

His driver pulled up to a building and I recognized it as the gun range.

"See you in a minute," Ray said to Don who did not exit the vehicle. "You sure you don't want to come?"

"I am okay. You two need to do this alone."

The three of us walked in the building and I was anxious to see why we were there. My face was still beyond swollen and my head didn't ache anymore thanks to the medication the hospital gave me. We followed behind Ray until we reached a window that had three pistols laying on the top. Ray nodded his head down the lane. What I saw brought the biggest smile to my face, and my hand naturally reached for my pistol. When Mocha saw it she smiled at me and grabbed her gun too.

"Ray," I said. "What the fuck kind of sick shit goes through your head?"

He laughed and grabbed his gun too. The light down their lane turned on and shined down on their target. Instead of having a paper target of some burglar or something, Khiron was bound naked to a chair with an apple in his mouth.

"Three hundred stacks to whoever blasts the apple from his mouth," Ray said, aiming his gun.

Khiron looked at us and several tears fell from his eyes. His eyes lingered on Mocha, and her raised gun shook slightly. He began screaming, but there was no point. It just came out muffled and nobody would hear him anyway. He fought against his binds, but it was no use. He knew he was about to die.

"Go!" Ray yelled.

Fuck that apple, I thought, and emptied my entire clip in his head.

"Bitch! Bitch! Bitch!" I yelled and watched as the force of our bullets splattered blood and tore him apart, literally. It felt so good.

I squeezed my trigger until it clicked, and by the time I reloaded there was really nothing more on his body to shoot.

"And that my friends," Ray started, "is how you kill a bitch nigga."

"He's dead," I heard the smile in Mocha's voice.

I looked at Ray. Although it had been over a year since I had seen him, I still knew his facial expressions. He set his gun down and nodded to me before he made his exit. Mocha set her gun down too, preparing to walk out, but I stopped her with my left arm and pushed her back. The gun still hung from my right hand, and I stared down at it for a second. The look on her face told me that she knew this was coming, but she was hoping it wouldn't.

"Sadie," she said, but really had nothing to say after. She knew what was up.

"You know why I have to do this, Mocha," I said to her, aiming my gun at her. "I can't let you live. You don't deserve to. You betrayed us, and death almost found us. You will never be able to be a part of The Last Kings again."

"But I don't want to be a part of it again. . . . I know I will never be welcomed back. I never wanted this life, Sadie."

"I know, but you still accepted it," I said, trying to ignore the lump forming in the back of my throat. It was getting harder and harder to look into her eyes by the second. "And if I don't do this now I'm positive that Devynn or Adrianna will."

I cocked my gun, and Mocha just stared at me with tears running freely from her eyes. I couldn't help it, I started to cry too. Mocha was my best friend who I loved like a sister, and even though she had committed the worst crime by breaking her loyalty to me, I still loved her. Love wasn't supposed to judge, but there was no telling when she would turn on me again. I couldn't trust her, and there was no way she would be able to get that back.

"Kings don't die," she said to me. "I love you, Say."

"I love you too, Mo. I will always love you," I said through my tears. "But you aren't a king . . . you were a mistake."

I shot my gun one time and saw the bullet enter the middle of her forehead and explode out the back due to the close range. Her head snapped back and when her body dropped, I felt like a piece of me died with her. I sobbed heavily and dropped the smoking gun. I couldn't even stare at her body, I just turned around and exited, knowing Ray would send somebody to clean it up later. When I was outside of the range I lost my composure and bent down and threw up everything that was in my stomach. My palms were on my knees and my body was convulsing when I felt a strong hand on my back.

"You had to do it, shorty," Ray said. "Or eventually somebody would have done it for you."

I just nodded my head, not wanting to talk. I just wanted to inhale as much fresh air as possible. He knew me, no matter how long he had been away. He forced me to stand up straight and held me while I sobbed into his shoulder. Murder had never touched me more than it had that very moment.

"I love you, Ray," I said to my cousin.

"I love you too, Say," he replied. "Come on, there's Don."

I wiped my eyes and walked slowly to the limo.

"Have you talked to Vinny?" I asked as we walked on the sidewalk to the advancing vehicle.

"Of course," Ray said.

"When are you copping?" I asked, knowing that since he was back The Last Kings could go back to its regularly scheduled program.

Ray looked at me and smiled sadly.

"I'm not," he said, and I didn't understand.

"What do you mean you're not?" I asked, stopping in my tracks.

"Exactly what it sounds like, little cousin."

"Then what did you come back for? To just leave again?"

"Business in Azura is booming," Ray tried to explain. "The product over there is perfection, and the money I make there is almost double what I could make here. I figured that with you here in Detroit, and now you have a new city, Atlanta, you can really be the leader of The Last Kings over here in the States. It's time to expand our shit. We are the physical binds that connect the Italian and the Dominican cartels. We're three major cartels, and now with Atlanta we are untouchable. You feeling me, Say?"

I was being selfish. I had just gotten him back to lose him again. Even though what he was saying made a lot of sense I didn't care, I wanted him to stay.

"You not gon' lose me shorty, you rich!" he said, reading my mind. "You can just hop on a plane whenever you want to and come see a nigga. And vice versa."

"Okay. . . ." I said, giving in. "You can leave again, but there is one stipulation. And you really don't have a choice but to say yes. I'm just trying to be nice and make it seem like you have an option, feel me?"

Ray laughed and looked at me.

"Niggas done bossed up on me. I feel you, Say. What's up, shorty?"

"Adrianna goes with you. And if you take A then you gotta take Dev too."

Ray smiled at the mention of Adrianna's name.

"You don't need them here?"

"I have a whole new team," I told him, smiling. "Plus Adrianna needs to be with the man she loves."

We embraced one more time before getting into the limo with our grandfather. That realization would take some getting used to. I knew Grandma Rae was stubborn, but to drop a rich man like Don and move to the hood proved that she was truly a brick house.

"So will you come home with us?" Don asked me once the vehicle began to move.

I shook my head gracefully.

"I wish I could," I said. "I have things to do here, though."

Ray smiled at me, nodding his approval.

"We have two new people joining us though," Ray said, and his voice trailed off.

I didn't hear their conversation, instead I got lost in my own thoughts until we reached the house. I put Mocha in the furthest part of my mind and thought of the great things that were to come. We could officially claim the city as ours. I went in first and saw everybody sitting in the living room. I smiled at them, not knowing how they were about to react.

"Umm, everybody . . ." I said. "I have somebody here who I'm sure you want to see."

If time could really stop, I would have experienced it right then and there, paused when Ray walked through the door. Adrianna dropped the glass she was holding and Legacy stood up so that he could squint his eyes. When her initial shock wore off, Adrianna ran like a track star to get to Ray.

"Ray!" she screamed and began to sob into his chest, clinging to him. "Ray!"

"What's up, ma?" he said, kissing her forehead. "I missed you, too."

Everybody went to surround him and ask him fifty million questions. I stepped back and let them do him. My cousin was back, and that was really all that mattered at that moment. I just wanted to see him smile. Adrianna looked at him with so much love that you would have thought his appearance was never altered. Instantly, my thoughts went to my own man. I missed Tyler already and couldn't wait for him to come back from Atlanta. The thought of actually being with the man I was in love with made me undoubtingly happy and complete. I knew when he came back though we would have a lot of work on our hands. It would take some months dedication to get Marie cleansed of the drugs in her system, and even more time to cater to the mental abuse she had suffered. But still she was more than willing to embark on that journey as long as Tyler was beside her. I felt a presence come up from behind me, and I turned around to see who was trying to creep up on me. When I saw that I was staring directly into Tyler's handsome face, my heart fluttered and the smile came naturally to my lips.

"Ty, I thought you left already," I said, genuinely happy he hadn't.

"Not without you, ma. I got tickets for a later flight," he said, pulling me close to him and giving me a deep kiss. "I packed your bag for you. I want you to come with me. After all of this I don't want to be without you for another minute."

I looked down and saw that he had indeed packed my things for me in a brown Louis Vuitton bag. I couldn't help it, the tears of joy made their presence known in my eyes. Tenderly, I ran a finger across his soft lips and then rested an open palm on his cheek.

"I love you, Tyler," I whispered up at him.

"I love you too, baby," he said, kissing me again. "We gotta go, though."

I looked back to Ray and saw he was watching us with a curious look in his eyes. I was waiting for him to say something. Instead, he looked at Tyler and gave him an approving smile and nod.

"Take care of my baby, bro," he said. "We've already died once."

I laughed, and Tyler picked up my bags.

"We'll be back tomorrow, don't worry," Tyler said to me. "With Marie here, the family will be complete."

I looked to Ray and he nodded, already knowing where my mind was at.

"I won't leave until you get back. I promise," he said to me, giving me the "Scouts Honor" sign.

"You ain't no fucking boy scout, boy!" I said, going up to him and giving him a big hug. "Promise me!"

"I just did," he said, but seeing the look in my eyes he kissed my forehead and shook his head. "I promise I'll stay here until you get back. Shit, if you want, I'll stand in this same spot for twenty-four hours."

"Stupid," I couldn't help but to laugh. I leaned back from him and looked at him once again, thanking God for bringing him back to me. "I love you, Ray. Adrianna, Legacy, Devynn, somebody just make sure this nigga don't do anything stupid, like die again while I'm gone. I don't think I can lose him twice."

I pulled away from Ray when I felt Tyler come behind me and he grabbed my hand so that he could lead me away to the door. We were almost out the door when I heard Ray call my name.

"Wassup?" I asked, turning back to face everybody.

"I love you, too," he said, and I smiled. "Kings don't die!"

"You're right," I winked at him and grabbed Tyler's hand. "Even in the grave, we live on forever!"

I smiled big at the sight of my new extended family. Blowing them all a kiss good-bye, I shut the door to the house, preparing to open up a new one to our future: The Last Kings.

Coming April 2017

by

C.N. Phillips

Deep:

A Twisted Tale of Deception

Prologue

"You can run . . . but you can't hide, Anna. I'm going to find youuuu!" An eerie voice rang out in the cold air.

Hearing the voice behind her made the panicked young woman run faster through the dimly lit concrete tunnel, feverishly checking behind her to make sure her stalker hadn't caught up to her. She had tears streaming down her face, and her heart was pumping with terror, but she willed her legs to go as quickly as they could carry her. It was a task, because whatever drug that was still in her system was slowing her down and making the world around her a big blur. She cried out when she heard the voice taunting her, because she knew the last place she wanted to be was in their clutches.

"Please leave me alone!" she yelled behind her. "Just let me go!"

Dry blood coated her body, and the back of her once pretty, long brown hair was matted. The more the drug wore off, the more the pain from her open wounds came back.

"Anna," the voice echoed from a ways behind her. "You aren't going to make it out of here. Why are you running? Just stop."

Anna sobbed but kept going. She didn't care that she was in lingerie or about the fact that she had black mascara running down her face. She didn't even care that the skin on her body was sliced up to the point that it looked like she was fresh off the set of a Texas Chainsaw Massacre *movie. The only thing that she was worried about was getting away from the psycho that had kidnapped her. Finally, she reached the end of the long hallway and fell into a tall wooden door. She felt the roughness of the wood under her cheek, and with shaky hands she gripped the cold, gold doorknob, trying to catch her breath. She knew that she was underground somewhere, she just prayed that the door was unlocked and that the room she was about to enter had a window. When she twisted the knob it easily turned, and without allowing another second go to waste she clambered through the open door. She glanced over her brown, exposed shoulder and saw a shadow rounding a corner a ways away before slamming it shut behind her. Turning the lock on the doorknob, she backed away from it, slowly trying to give her eyes time to adjust to the darkness of the room. The air was stuffy, making it hard for her to breathe, and the stench in there was almost unbearable, but she tried not to let that faze her.*

"Window," she muttered to herself once she could see slightly. "I need a window. Please God let me find a window."

On the floor, there was a light that could only be given by the moon and Anna's heart fluttered with hope. She followed the light, ignoring the cold of the stone floor under her bare feet, until she finally found the source in which the light was coming from. There was a window on the far wall, and she saw that it was just big enough for her to get through it. Underneath it there was a box that she hurriedly stood on to reach what she hoped would be her cavalry. Anna reached her hand up and tried to unlatch the hook, but for some reason, no matter how hard she tugged it wouldn't budge. Behind her she heard the doorknob begin to jiggle, and her eyes darted toward the ground underneath the door. There was a shadow moving there, and Anna began to sob. She was so close to evading her captor, all she had to do was open the window. She stood shakily on her tip toes so that she could get a better look at what she was doing. What she saw almost made her scream. There was a pad lock on the other side of the window; there was no way to open it without a key.

"No!" She whimpered in disbelief. Balling her hand into a fist she tried to hit the window, but she was far too weak to cause any real damage.

Anna stepped down from the box so that she could find something to bust through the glass with, but it was too late. The door was wide open behind her and a sinister silhouette stood there, holding a sharp machete that seemed to gleam in the light. Anna knew there was nowhere to run, but still she was not ready to meet the fate staring her dead in the face. Defeated, Anna dropped to her knees and she wept.

"P-please don't kill me," Anna begged through her sobs. "I don't want to die. Please don't kill me!"

Instead of responding, the silhouette walked slowly toward her, coming out of the shadows. Her figure was finally visible and the heels on her feet clicked with each step. When she finally reached Anna, she knelt down and put her red lips next to the trembling young woman's ear.

"I told you not to run," she whispered into Anna's ear. "And you did."

"P-please," Anna begged in a barely audible voice. "I don't want to die."

"You are the only one who ran," the woman put the cold metal of the machete against the nape of Anna's neck. "So why would I kill you? You, my dear, have heart."

With quivering lips, Anna looked up into the empty eyes of the person who had taken her entire life away.

Freedom had been her desire for the past two weeks, and she couldn't believe that she was going to be granted that. Maybe it had all been a test. A sick test.

"Y-you're going to let me go?" Anna breathed.

"I'm not going to kill you," the woman said and chuckled at the naivety of the girl before her. She gently gripped the bottom of Anna's chin and stared coldly into her eyes. "But you will never be free . . . you belong to me. And this?" The woman motioned to the machete and placed it in Anna's hand before standing to her feet. "That is yours. Follow me, you have work to do."

Chapter 1

The sound of automatic rounds being fired plagued the night air as two thieves ran for their lives. Each was dressed in all black and had a duffle bag on their shoulder. Heads ducked down, they pushed their feet to go as fast as they could. Bullets ricocheted off of the concrete and found homes in cars parked on the street of the neighborhood they were running through. The neighborhood they were in was lit by the street lights and people were peeking through their windows to see what was going on outside of their homes.

"Move! Move!" one of the thieves shouted to a young woman who had just stepped out of her car, clutching a bag of groceries.

The warning came too late. She was clipped by multiple bullets in the center of her chest and blasted off of her feet. There was no time to be sad at the innocent life lost, because the assailants running after them weren't letting up. The thieves were forced to make a quick right turn into somebody's open gate and run through their neatly trimmed yard. The two lucked up, because the backyard of the house led to the alley where they had parked their getaway vehicle. The first thief dropped the duffle bag they were holding to the ground while still running full speed in front of the second. They jumped the fence effortlessly and waited for their partner to throw both duffle bags over before they too followed suit. They continued their pace toward where the 2010 all black Chevy Tahoe was parked in the shadows.

"They're getting close!" the first thief said, jumping and sliding over the hood of the truck.

"Hurry up and start the truck then!" the second thief yelled, yanking open the passenger door and jumping in before slamming the door back.

Looking to the right, they saw the young thugs toting their automatic weapons and jumping the fence that led to the alley.

"Go! Go!" the second thief said and ducked their head just in time because the thugs wasted no time in unloading their bullets into the vehicle.

The windows on the right side of the truck were instantly shattered, and the second thief ducked and threw their arms over their head. Rapid fire was sounding as the thugs were unleashing all of their ammunition into the truck. With still hands, the thief in the driver's seat turned the key and started the engine. Driving was slightly hard due to the fact that both of their heads were ducked, but the driver went based off of memory. Whipping the steering wheel all the way left, the driver hit a U-turn and mashed on the gas. They made a swift getaway before their opponents were able to get too close to the vehicle. They kept their heads ducked low until they were sure they were out of range of the guns shooting at them.

"Hit that right," the thief in the passenger's seat guided the driver with expertise through North Omaha. "I parked off of Twenty-fourth and Lake by where the Blue Lion used to be, so take the back streets."

"Why would you park so far from the hit?"

"So if they followed us it would give us more time to lose them. Just shut up and drive, dude, you always have something to say."

The tension in the car wasn't uncommon after a job that led to a near death experience for the pair. After they were absolutely positive that they were not followed they began their route to where the second car was parked. It didn't take too long to reach a neighborhood not too far from the vehicle. They parked the shot up truck in front of an abandoned house and wiped down the inside of it before grabbing the two duffle bags. It wasn't the first time the two had ditched a car, so they both knew the drill, nothing was left behind. Shielded by the night sky, they ran the two blocks to the gold 2002 Chevy Impala they had stolen earlier that day.

"What time is it?"

"Almost ten," the second thief said, finally removing the face mask. Starting the car, they pulled off from the curb. "Take your mask and hoodie off so we can dump them on the way home."

"Sometimes I swear you're the big sister and not me, Rhonnie."

Rhonnie smirked at her big sister as she drove up Lake Street.

"You know, I've always been the more responsible one. Two years means nothing, Ahli."

"Whatever. Just get us home. Turn on some Eric Bellinger. His voice always calms me down after a night like this."

Rhonnie did as she was told and turned on her sister's favorite artist. Although she wanted to discuss the contents of the bags they had in the backseat, she knew it wasn't the time or the place. She knew that their father had sent them on the mission for a reason, but usually they robbed people of cash. Not—

"Stop thinking so much," Ahli interrupted Rhonnie's thoughts with her head back and her eyes closed. She already knew what was going on through her sister's nosey head. "We'll ask him when we get home."

As always, Ahli was in her head, but Rhonnie couldn't do anything but sigh and continue driving. She was trying to get back out west as fast as she could because she knew their current area would soon be swarming with cops and that was the last thing that they needed. They rode, listening to the soft croons coming from the speakers for the next thirty minutes until they finally reached their destination. Hitting the garage door remote on the Impala's visor, Rhonnie pulled the car into the garage of the vast, five-bedroom brick house. She planned to dump the car early the next day, however, at that moment, they needed to sit still for a while. The girls grabbed the bags from the back seat of the car and walked inside of the house, but not before shutting the garage door behind them.

"Dad!" Rhonnie yelled out not able to contain herself. She didn't care if he was sleep or not. "Dad!"

"Chill, NaNa," Ahli said, shooting her little sister a look as they made their way into the living room of their home.

"Fuck that," Rhonnie said, using a word she rarely pulled from her vocabulary.

She plopped down on the black leather couch and pulled her black hoodie over her head, revealing a white tank top under. She kicked the black Timberlands off of her feet and crossed her arms. Her eyes were focused on the spiral staircase by the foyer of the house, and they stayed there until she saw the familiar Ralph Lauren house slippers making their way down the steps.

When Quinton Malone entered the living room he had a smile on his face as soon as he saw both of the duffle bags on the black marble coffee table.

"Good work," he told them, but his smile soon faded when his eyes met his younger daughter's. "Why the long face, NaNa?"

Rhonnie took a deep breath before she mustered up the courage to come at her father in any form of disagreement. She glanced at Ahli, who in turn just shrugged her shoulders.

So much for back up, Rhonnie thought.

"Daddy, why you got us stealing coke?" Rhonnie finally asked. "You had us getting shot at for cocaine! Since when did you become a drug dealer?"

Quinton figured that the question was coming, so he was prepared for it. He sat down in the Lazy Boy diagonal from the couch that his daughters were sitting on. He observed them and saw the sweat still glistening on their foreheads and the tiredness in their eyes. He felt a small pang of guilt, but not enough to regret sending them to do the job. It wasn't the first time that they had been shot at, and he was sure that it wouldn't be the last, either. He stared his daughter in the eyes until she blinked before speaking.

"I never said I was," he spoke in a smooth voice, but his children knew him well enough to recognize the deadly undertone. "The contents in those bags are probably only worth fifty thousand dollars combined. I have a buyer who is willing to pay double that."

"Sounds a lot like drug dealing," Rhonnie said, raising her eyebrow at her father. Although the last thing she wanted to do was disrespect him, she had to let him know that she didn't agree with him. "If you would have told us what we were really jacking, I would have never gone."

"Exactly the reason I didn't say anything. I need you both to trust me."

"Daddy, having that in the house is probably the dumbest thing we have ever done. I don't want to be around it. Period. And you got me risking my life for it."

"This is an opportunity that I can't pass up . . . can you?"

"If I would have known I was going to be robbing a house full of people with automatic weapons, I definitely would have passed," Rhonnie shot back, not letting up on her dad.

Quinton sighed and rubbed his large hand down the neatly trimmed beard on his face. Whereas Ahli was more like their mother, Rhonnie was just like him. From her bullheaded mind frame to her stubborn attitude, she was definitely Quinton Jr. However, he knew she had a get-money mentality just like him, so that was what he honed in on at that moment.

"So you're going to let the job you just did go unpaid for? A'ight, go drop those bags off somewhere then, miss out on all of that money."

To that, Rhonnie had no comment. She had become accustomed to being able to drive any kind of car she wanted and being able to wear whatever designer she saw fit. Instead of responding to her father, she just looked at her feet.

"When do they expect us to deliver?" Ahli finally chimed in. "Because Rhonnie is right, we need to get that stuff out of the house as soon as possible, Daddy. You know you just got off papers."

She stared into her father's warm face and noticed that he must have gotten his brush cut lined up and his beard trimmed while they were out handling business earlier that day. He was looking debonair and sophisticated, even in his night clothes.

"In two days," Quinton told her clasping his hands together. "The drop happens at one o'clock on Friday. In Miami."

"Miami!" Rhonnie exclaimed. "That drive is like twenty-four hours!"

"Twenty-three," Quinton corrected her. "And that's exactly why we need to rest up, because we are leaving first thing in the morning."

Ahli wanted the work gone, but she didn't say that she wanted to move it that soon. The two girls would barely have enough time to recoup from the job they had just done before they would be on another one. She knew better than to argue with her father; she had more respect for him than that. Rhonnie, on the other hand, just couldn't seem to contain her thoughts.

"Tomorrow? How does Uncle Lance even know these people are good for their word?" Rhonnie asked skeptically.

"Because your Uncle Lance has never steered me wrong. Ever," Quinton winked at Rhonnie. "Now shut up and listen."

Both Rhonnie and Ahli got quiet knowing that their father was about to brief them on how things would go the next day. He explained to them that they would take two cars and leave thirty minutes apart. He told them that the drugs would be hidden in the car with them, just to stay on the safe side of things. Although he could legally leave the state, Quinton knew he had eyes on him. The last thing he needed was to get pulled over with two bags of bricks in his vehicle. He knew that what they were doing was risky, but he figured that the two of them would be all right as long as Ahli drove. He informed them that he had already booked them separate rooms at the Hilton. When they got there, they were to park in the back of the hotel and check in like normal, but leave the duffle bags of drugs in the car. Afterward they were to shower, get dressed and go back to the car and wait for him. From there they would go and make the drop.

"Sounds easy enough," Ahli said, nodding her head, seemingly pleased with the plan.

"They always seem easy," Rhonnie said, standing to her feet and stretching her arms wide. "But are they ever easy? No. I'm going to bed since we have to be back up in like six hours. Night, y'all."

She didn't wait for them to say it back before she made her exit. Quinton sighed and shook his head.

"I didn't want this for you girls," he said aloud and mostly to himself.

"I know, Daddy." Ahli shrugged her shoulders. "But it's what we gotta do. Nobody knew mommy was going to die. I understand why you do what you have to do. And I don't mind going in your place."

"Tell that to your sister."

"She's young," Ahli said. "She wants to enjoy her youth. Just give her a couple of days and she'll be all right."

She stood up and planted a kiss on Quinton's forehead before she, too, bounded up the stairs, leaving him lost in his thoughts.

"Sister, wake up," a voice evaded Rhonnie's dreams.

She groaned and tried to roll over and bury her body deeper into her plush lavender covers. It literally felt like she had just closed her eyes and that sleep hadn't even found her yet.

"Fihh muh minutes," she mumbled into her pillow.

"No!" she heard a stern voice say, and then felt the covers being yanked off of her. "It's already five thirty in the morning. Get up. I'm trying to get this shit done and over with."

"Ahli!" Rhonnie yelled as the gust of cold air hit her bare legs. Her eyes popped open, and sure enough, there was her big sister standing in front of her, wide awake. Ahli was fully dressed in a form fitting T-shirt and a pair of Levi skinny jeans that hugged her hips and made her thighs look extra thick. "I'm sleepy!"

"Sleep in the car," Ahli said and threw some clothes at her little sister.

Thursday morning came faster than Rhonnie had anticipated, and getting out of her comfortable bed felt like torture. Rhonnie looked up at her sister again and took in her appearance. Her kinky, long curly hair was pulled back into a neat ponytail, her mocha skin was clear and smooth, and her eyelashes were long and luscious as if she had put mascara on them. It was apparent that her sister had been up for a while.

"Fuck," she mumbled to herself and sat up. Her eyelids were still heavy, but she knew with Ahli hovering over her there was no going back to sleep. The smell of food cooking evaded her nostrils and her mouth instantly began to water. "Is Daddy up?"

"Yea, he's downstairs," Ahli said. "He made breakfast for us and he said he has one more thing to tell us before we leave. I already packed your bag, so don't worry about it. Fucking with you we wouldn't leave until noon."

Rhonnie grinned sheepishly before she stood up from her bed and stumbled slightly. Using her knuckles, she wiped her eyes, trying to force herself to wake up.

"Okay, I'll meet you downstairs. Let me get in the shower."

"I'm giving you twenty minutes tops." Ahli gave her little sister a knowing look. "If I have to come back up here and get you, it's problems."

"Okay, *mother*."

When Ahli left the room Rhonnie grabbed the clothes that were thrown at her. A simple pair of jeans, a cotton Ralph Lauren T-shirt, a pair of boy-short panties with the tag still attached, and a pair of socks. Rhonnie smiled to herself. Although Ahli was only two years older, she had really stepped up to the motherly role when their mother died, years ago. Ahli was so busy being strong for everybody else that Rhonnie knew that it would be messed up to ever give her a hard time about anything. So most times she listened to her sister because most times she was right. Rhonnie couldn't count how many bullets should have entered her body on one hand anymore if it weren't for her big sister looking out. She snatched up the clothing and made her way to the bathroom that was in her bedroom so that she could prepare for the day. She spent ten minutes in the shower, relishing in the feeling of the hot water smacking her body. Once she was done she dried off, applied her favorite lotion, and then attempted to do something with her long, thick hair. When all else failed, she ended up simply mimicking the pony tail that her sister was wearing, but swooping her edges more neatly than Ahli had. When she was done she studied herself in the mirror. She was a perfect mix of both of her parents. She had her mother's doe-like chestnut brown eyes, sharp cheekbones, and smooth caramel skin. From her father, she got his grade of hair, full lips, and his smile.

Knowing that she was about to go over the time limit that Ahli had given her, she hurried out of her room and down the stairs toward the kitchen. She heard her dad going over the events of the next day with Ahli once more, and when he saw her enter the kitchen he smiled her way and motioned for her to take a seat next to her sister. There was already a plate in front of the chair he motioned for her to go to. She noticed that their plates had already been dug into, but she didn't care. She was just happy her food was still hot, since even if it was cold she was still going to eat. Her dad threw down in the kitchen.

"Good morning, Daddy," Rhonnie said, kissing him on his forehead and snagging a piece of his bacon before sitting down. She took in his outfit and saw that he was dressed comfortably to travel. Even when he was dressed down in a Nike jogging suit outfit with all white Nike Roshes, he was fly. "When we leaving?"

"Right after you eat," He told her.

"Okay," she said and then turned to her sister. "Why were you up so early? I was tired as hell after last night."

"I know, Big Hungry," Ahli said, reaching out and brushing a bacon crumb from her lip. "That's why I took the initiative to get up and dump that Impala we were in last night."

Rhonnie grinned sheepishly at her sister before dousing her scrambled eggs with Louisiana hot sauce and taking a big bite.

"Thanks, sister."

"Uh-huh."

Quinton waited patiently for Rhonnie to finish her food before he placed the two slightly weighted black boxes from his lap and placed them on the wooden kitchen table. He saw his daughters' eyes light up the way they always did when he bought them gifts, and he slid a box in front of each of them.

"Go ahead, open them."

Ahli and Rhonnie wasted no time snatching the tops off of their boxes. When they saw the contents of the boxes, they didn't know whether to be excited or skeptical. Rhonnie took hers out and eyed the black Ruger LC9s in her hand. Ahli did the same with her Ruger SR45, and the both looked up at their father after a few moments.

"It was time that you got new ones," was all he said before he stood up and grabbed their empty plates. "Since y'all always want to wear those tight ass jeans, those are compact enough to fit in your purses."

Ahli nodded and stood up too, glancing at the clock on the wall.

"Come on NaNa," she motioned to her sister. "It's time to get this show on the road."

Rhonnie was still eyeing her new toy and shook her head.

"Great . . . we're traveling across the world with drugs and guns. Just great."